The Impossible Wish

Christine Nolfi

Dear Eloise)
Thank you for joining
Liberty Ladies. It's so
great getting to know you.
with love,
Christine

Author website: www.christinenolfi.com
Cover Design: Valentine-Design.com

*For my son Jameson, who has uncommon courage
And Barry, who always gets it right*

Acknowledgments

Special thanks to my brilliant editor Wendy Reis, who has lovingly edited the entire Liberty Series. Her patience, humor and guidance make the long days of writing a joy.
My gratitude goes to Linda Weber and Philomena Callan for reading early drafts. Ladies, your comments kept the story flowing and provided much needed support. I'd also like to thank my literary assistant Ravina Kurian for keeping the promotion schedule running smoothly while I worked. Without her, the time I dedicate to writing would sadly decrease.

Special thanks goes to Renaissance woman and award-winning author and graphic designer Kathleen Valentine of Valentine-Design.com. Kathleen, I not only appreciate your unique art direction for *Wish;* I value your friendship as well.

Lastly, I send my heartfelt thanks to USA Today Bestselling Author Bette Lee Crosby for her wit, wisdom and sage advice, and to my husband Barry—my love and greatest champion.

Chapter 1

The way Birdie Kaminsky saw it, paradise lasted three months, three weeks and five days.

Shimmying into her jeans, she peered at the clothing flung across the floor by the cyclone of her temper. Nothing made her fiancé and the co-owner of the recently opened *Liberty Post* crazier than a disordered living space, which probably explained why she felt inclined to treat their new digs like a patch of Oklahoma's tornado alley.

She'd grown tired of his pithy comments about how neatness counts, and the work schedule he insisted they keep was a killer. Who in their right mind rose at dawn for anything but sex or a light snack before heading back to the Land of Nod? Or played interior decorator after a grueling day of work? Last night Hugh had painted their bedroom until well after midnight, ensuring they both stayed up too late.

If this was how the honest half lived, she should've read the fine print.

Morning light covered the floor in a blinding pattern. She stumbled through the glare, kicking a heap of clothing out of the way and sending the lighter lingerie aloft. One of her *Victoria's Secret* bras skimmed the wall, collecting a spatter of eggshell blue paint. The destruction of cherished lingerie combined with the early hour sent her temper into the stratosphere.

"Hugh!" she bellowed in the general direction of the living room. "Get moving. We have the stupid interview you scheduled for this morning."

"Interviews, as in plural." Hugh Schaeffer followed his irritable response into the bedroom. "The second one is this afternoon."

His deliciously dark eyes scanned the mess flung across the floor. Clothes, a notepad, the Chinese takeout boxes Birdie had taken to bed when he'd chosen to sleep on the couch for the fourth night running—the floor was an obstacle course of debris.

She offered a smile as sweet as a poisoned apple. "Now, don't say it. I'll clean after we get home tonight. Right now I'm busy prying my eyes open."

"That's what you said yesterday and the day before. Face it, Birdie. You have the domestic skills of a toddler."

"Can I at least grab some coffee before you start badgering me?" It seemed best to enter the fray caffeinated.

Hugh leaned against the doorjamb. "There's no brew. I couldn't find the coffee pot beneath the crap you left in the kitchen."

It didn't take a genius to know what he was thinking—their new digs deserved TLC.

Together they'd purchased the barn on the outskirts of town right after Christmas. They'd renovated the main floor for the new *Liberty Post* daily newspaper and added a love den upstairs that he now undoubtedly viewed as a house of horrors.

They'd rebuilt the massive second floor to include a gourmet kitchen for the domestically inclined Hugh, a living room with gorgeous skylights in the vaulted ceiling, and a spacious bedroom meant to become a lover's paradise but which was more accurately described as a demon's roost, Birdie being the demon.

She snatched up her paint-spattered bra. "I'm not going to the second interview." She held the lingerie out for his inspection. "Look what you've done. My favorite bra is ruined."

"You have twenty favorite bras. Since you've come into your inheritance you've done nothing but shop. Keep it up and Saks will open a store in backwoods Liberty, Ohio."

Finding a comeback proved impossible, probably because he was correct.

The windfall *had* gone to her head. Last December she'd inherited a bag of rubies appraised at just shy of one million dollars. The gems were tucked away at the bank, but she'd used a handful for collateral to open the newspaper with Hugh and embark on a clothing feeding frenzy that would do a piranha proud.

True, the women at The Second Chance Grill had warned her, sometimes subtly but often bluntly, that money could change a woman in unbecoming ways. Listening to their advice wasn't the same as acting on it.

Besides, Birdie wasn't ready to put an end to the shopping extravaganza, not after spending all of her thirty-two years living by her wits and going without the creature comforts other people took for granted. Well, other *rich* people. Most of her friends in town were rich in character but didn't have much in the way of cash.

"We'll drive to Bell Corners after we get the mayor's comments on the new zoning committee," Hugh was saying. "You're not ditching this afternoon's interview with the women's group."

"I'll pretend to care about the mayor's zoning laws but I'm not interviewing those women afterward. Remember the skinny chick with the dark hair? Last weekend at The Second Chance Grill, I heard her muttering about me. *Ella está ávida de fama.* I looked it up on

Google—she thinks I'm greedy for fame."

"Maybe she's envious of your Gucci handbag. Most women in town could put their kids through private school on what you pay for glitz."

"So I've bought some new stuff."

"What about the Corvette? It doesn't exactly blend in with the beaters rattling around Liberty Square. This isn't Palm Beach. People think you're showing off."

"I bought a new car. Big deal." She'd never before owned wheels, but the banana yellow Vette hadn't worked out as planned. All winter she'd hydroplaned through snow, scaring pedestrians off sidewalks and doing unintended wheelies on Highway 6. Thank God spring had arrived. "It's not a crime to own a nice car."

"That's the problem. You miss crime, picking pockets and living on the fly. You haven't exactly turned over a new leaf, Birdie."

The comment landed a bull's eye on her heart. "I don't miss my former life. Who would? I now own half of a local newspaper. I live with a permanent roof over my head and don't have to dash out of a store if the cops walk in. Being legal suits me fine." She paused by the wall and sniffed. The blue paint was still tacky, sending fumes across the bedroom in nauseating waves. "Why did you pick this color? It's infantile."

Hugh dragged his hand through his ebony hair. "I thought light blue would be calming. You know—for a bedroom. *Our* bedroom. If I'd been a psychic, I would've chosen fire engine red."

"What's that supposed to mean?"

"All we do is fight about the *Liberty Post* or who should handle the more boring interviews," he replied. The regret in his voice dug the arrow deeper into her emotions. "We bicker about how to decorate our new home, or squabble over new hires for the newspaper's staff. Mostly we fight our way around the problems in our relationship."

She didn't like when Hugh's voice went soft around the edges to work its way beneath the armor she'd spent years layering over her heart. The truth he spoke roused her conscience from its preferred slumber, making her consider how her actions affected others—affected him mostly because she needed him like she'd never needed anyone before. The thought intimidated her as much as the early morning hour.

"Lighten up, will you? There's nothing wrong with our relationship." She grabbed mascara and blush, and did quick work on her face. When Hugh crossed his arms, unconvinced, she added, "Okay, so we've hit a few speed bumps. Couples don't always get along."

"That's true, but you're not even trying. You're temperamental, moody—you should be on top of the world. Most people never come into money. Those who do are usually happy about it. Good fortune isn't supposed to bring out the worst in people."

"Meaning it has with me?"

Hugh tossed over the hairbrush and she ran it through her hair. Suffering beneath his frigid inspection wasn't easy, the warmth gone from his eyes, the affection. Had he fallen out of love with her? The possibility sent anxiety snapping through her.

Setting down the brush, she faced him. "Here's the thing," she said, trying for a casual note that belied the worry stalking her. "I'm waiting for the axe to fall."

"What axe?"

"Come on. You know what I mean."

He released a sigh of frustration. "Birdie, I don't," he said. "Why don't you clue me in?"

She did, hating the way it made her feel small— maybe worthless. "I was born under an unlucky star," she admitted. "Look at my mother. She's conned decent people across the U.S. She's racked up misery from Maine to California."

11

Hugh digested the explanation with commendable calm. "Just because you were raised by a criminal doesn't mean you're destined for failure. Forget the past and create something better."

"I was raised in a family of con men and grifters. All I know is how to live by my wits."

"So you're scared. Who isn't? If you're waiting for a happiness guarantee, guess what? Life doesn't work that way."

"You aren't listening." The waver in her voice made her unaccountably angry. "Deep down, I can't shake the feeling that none of this will last. Why not live it up while I can? Sure, it seems like my life is perfect now, settled—it's an illusion. Somehow, it'll all fall apart."

"Like you're destined for disaster? By fate or . . . whatever?"

"Exactly."

Hugh's brows lifted. Pity worked across his face or maybe it was sadness. It was hard to tell behind the tears blurring her vision. He sat heavily on the side of the bed and dropped his elbows on his knees, weaving his fingers together as if in prayer. Only she should be the one praying because she sensed something entering the room, a haunting regret. It threatened the bond they'd forged during the last months.

"Birdie." He hesitated. When he tried again, she knew the words came at a cost. "Ever since I fell in love with you, I've wanted to believe I could help you find a better way to live. You've found real family here in Liberty, relatives who'll stand by you no matter what. You have every reason to believe the world offers more than the suffering you've known. But the way you've been acting toward me—toward all of us—it's like you're trying to drive everyone away. If it seems like your luck can't last, maybe *you're* the one destroying it."

"But I want to be happy."

"A closetful of clothes won't make you happy. A new car won't either."

"You mean I'm superficial." Another direct jab. She tried to take it with grace. If she refused to hear him out, how could she pretend they had a future together? A tart comment hovered on her lips but she bit it back.

Evidently he wasn't finished laying it on. "You're trying to fill a hole in your heart with expensive baubles and trips to the mall. Maybe you can't feel contentment because it's outside your emotional repertoire." Hugh cut off, his mouth twitching and his eyes gleaming with the kind of heartache she didn't want him to feel. "Maybe it's too late for you to learn."

Drumming up a suitable retort proved impossible.

No, she didn't understand contentment or how people nested together in families and close relationships, and let the love they cherished see them through good times and bad. It seemed like blind optimism, an unnatural order in a chaotic world.

Didn't half of all couples end up divorced? Didn't parents sacrifice to raise kids who then moved three states away? People in Liberty seemed different and she wanted to believe they were; some families housed three generations under one roof. There were people like Theodora Hendricks with cherished relatives strung across Jeffordsville County in a tapestry of love. Birdie was now part of Theodora's family and a law-abiding resident of town. Yet it was impossible to shake the cynicism knit deep in her bones.

Rising, Hugh stuffed his hands into the pockets of his jeans. "You're going with me to *both* interviews today. We're on a tight deadline." When she began to protest, he added, "We're business partners. You aren't bailing out. After we finish, I'll drop you off."

"You're not coming home with me?" She wondered if he'd lined up a third interview today, something she'd forgotten.

For a moment he stared at her before turning on his heel. She followed him down the hall.

In the living room, the pillows on the taupe leather couch were neatly arranged. The sheaf of papers she'd littered across the glass coffee table was stacked beside her iPad and the fashion magazines that had become an addiction. Outside the bank of windows, April sunshine washed the green rolling hills.

By the door, Hugh's luggage waited.

He picked it up. "I'm moving in with the Perini's."

The announcement hovered between them for a terrible moment. "You're staying with Mary and Anthony?" Her knees turned rubbery and she leaned against the wall.

"And Blossom, yes. They said I'm welcome to one of their spare bedrooms for as long as I want. They won't tell anyone, Birdie." He released a brittle laugh. "If that's what you're worried about."

Disbelief whirled through her. "You're leaving me?"

He yanked open the door. From over his shoulder he said, "I've made a commitment to build the *Liberty Post* with you, and I will. The rest of it? I'm not sure anymore."

Inside the renovated barn and home of the new *Liberty Post,* Snoops Keeley tapped the computer screen in disbelief. The data blinking before her didn't make sense. A low, whistling breath streamed from her lips.

Behind purple-framed glasses, her black bean eyes snapped. Maybe she was only in junior high but as the town's smartest resident with computers and social media, she was a cyber-force worthy of respect.

Last year when her best friend had been dodging the Grim Reaper and in need of a bone marrow transplant, Snoops had built websites and blogged relentlessly to draw national media attention to the cause. People from across the U.S. donated enough money for Blossom Perini's medical expenses and then some. Now Blossom wasn't just healthy—she was the youngest reporter in Ohio. Maybe she wasn't a journalist exactly, but her online blog for the *Liberty Post* was read in lots of cool places like Miami, Los Angeles and Seattle.

Snoops leaned close to the computer monitor with an icky feeling pooling in her stomach. All of the grown-ups were out chasing stories, including the new reporters Hugh had hired. They'd left Snoops and Blossom in charge for an hour, mostly because calls rarely came in this late in the day. The new receptionist would start next week. Snoops looked around helplessly.

The barn had a new oak floor but the faint odor of horse poo drifted past her offended nose. She liked horses all right, but wished they hadn't left evidence of their occupancy in a newsroom now serving a three-county area and a large online following. At her knees, Blossom's golden retriever squirmed.

"Sweetcakes, stop bugging me." Something was wrong with the files, and she needed to focus. "Stupid dog. Go away."

"Don't yell at my dog." Blossom, busy typing two desks away, puffed up her cheeks then blew out a stream of air. "How many times do I have to tell you? Sweetcakes bugs you because you haul food around like a gypsy. She wants whatever's stashed in your pocket."

"I lug food because I eat when I'm nervous."

Or worried—the computer files looked like they'd been messed with. A data snatch-and-grab was enough to have her withdrawing a sandwich from the roomy folds of her sweatshirt. She bit with relish. The yummy aroma of roast beef and cheddar made Sweetcakes quiver.

Not that Snoops presently cared about Blossom's dog.

From the looks of it someone had crept past the

firewall, a notion so surprising she sat blinking in a desperate attempt to reboot her brain. Birdie's middle name was deleted from one form. Her work history had a weird new entry for a clothing store in New Mexico, and some of the articles she'd written were missing—only the date of entry remained. Was this a hoax? Or something worse?

The second possibility sprouted goosebumps on her arms. She tossed down the sandwich and sent her fingers streaming across the keyboard.

Blossom spun around in her chair. "You don't look so good. What are you working on?"

"I'm tracking something. Don't bug me."

"I like bugging you. It gives my life purpose."

"Blossom—"

Opening a second screen on the computer, Snoops made a split second decision that left a bitter taste in her mouth. Some things were sacred, and she wasn't supposed to even know the password. Of course, only someone as careless as Birdie would leave the password Free2roaM in a file entitled *My Stuff*. Jotting it down, she logged into the bank where the *Liberty Post* sent payroll.

Corkscrew curls bouncing, Blossom leapt from her chair. "Are you looking at bank accounts?" She peered at the columns of numbers glowing on the screen. "You don't have permission!"

"I have to look. The website was compromised, and the hack targeted Birdie. What if someone also broke into her account?"

"You can't snoop in her private stuff. We aren't even supposed to work here. We're in junior high."

"Are you for real? Without me, this place would operate with typewriters." She tipped her head at the window, and the green hills surrounding the barn. "This isn't exactly a metropolitan area. There isn't anyone else with my skill set."

The ready defense didn't placate Blossom. "What if you get us in trouble?" she asked.

"Since when do you care about trouble?" Mischief flowed in her best friend's veins. Blossom had collected enough detentions from the school principal to paper the walls of her bedroom. "I have to check this out. It looks like someone hacked the system."

"Geez, are you looking at Birdie *and* Hugh's bank accounts?"

Birdie and Hugh had sealed their engagement within days of hiring some part-time staff and opening the *Liberty Post*. They spent most of their time chasing stories. The rest of the time they traded barbs and kisses—Snoops wished they'd stop fighting and get married already.

"Hugh's accounts look okay. Birdie's stuff is a different story." She studied the withdrawals blinking on the screen. "Look. Someone has been taking money from her checking account."

Blossom lifted her shoulders in a careless shrug. "It's Birdie's account. She's making the withdrawals."

"Guess again. She doesn't know how to *use* checking."

"Sure she does. It's a rule. Grownups learn everything about money."

"Trust me, she's clueless. She dumped money into checking and left it there. She lives on cash."

"That's dumb. Why open an account and not use it?"

"To get Hugh to stop bugging her."

The way he tried to teach Birdie *was* sweet. Her previous life hadn't prepared her for basic stuff, like dealing with alarm clocks or staying put in one place. But she was making progress.

Blossom twirled one of her curls. "I don't care if Birdie opens ten accounts," she said. "It won't stop Hugh from getting on her case. Nagging is his favorite pastime."

"He's only trying to teach her to be responsible." Actually it was cool how Birdie had lived by her wits before opening the *Liberty Post.* Now she'd gone straight, but she hadn't figured out how to use a bank for anything but breaking and entering. Well, maybe her past didn't involve bank robberies, but she *had* been a pickpocket. "Someone's been taking out small amounts of cash from her checking. Twenty, thirty bucks at a time."

Blossom flashed pearly teeth. "If it were me, I'd take it all," she said. Splotches of red climbed her cheeks. "Kidding."

"Remind me *not* to teach you how to access the bank."

"Like I want to learn. Math is boring." Blossom snatched the sandwich from the desk and tossed it into her dog's waiting chompers. Sweetcakes ran off, tail wagging a victory salute. "I don't get it, *Sensei.* Why is someone snatching small amounts of dough from Birdie?"

"To see if she's watching her bank account. Small withdrawals are easy to miss."

"What about the other accounts? I got paid last week." Blossom hung over the desk. "Tell me no one has touched my money. I'm saving for an iPad. If someone has taken my loot there'll be hell to pay."

"It isn't loot if you earned it. And I already checked. The other accounts are fine."

"Then why are you worried?"

"Grabbing small amounts of cash from Birdie's account is one thing. What if someone goes hog wild and messes up the newspaper?"

Fingers dancing across the keyboard, Snoops darted in and out of the newspaper's main files. She found a photograph missing in one file and half of an article deleted in another. The hacker knew what he was doing—none of the altered files were of current news stories.

Someone was playing around with reports

published weeks ago by Birdie, the kind of stuff you'd never find unless you consciously looked for it. Not that the prospect of someone tampering with old files made Snoops feel any better. Tomorrow the cyberpunk might alter the *Liberty Post's* online edition ten minutes before it went live. Or tamper with the print edition before it was transmitted to the printer.

A sharp poke in the ribs nudged her from her thoughts. "What should we do?" Blossom asked. She began biting her nails. "Call Birdie and Hugh?"

"You know the rule. We aren't supposed to bug them when they're working a story. Not unless it's an emergency." Which this was, but Snoops had a better idea. She grabbed her backpack from beneath the desk and slid her laptop inside. "Close up here, okay? Don't forget to lock the door on your way out."

"Where are you going?"

"To The Second Chance Grill."

"Without me? You know I'm always game for a chocolate sundae with extra sprinkles."

"You promised your dad you'd be home for dinner, remember?"

"What about *your* parents?"

"They're visiting my grandma. They'll never know I'm late." Snoops puffed out her chest. Even if she was a year short of the official teenage years, she knew when she smelled the stinky odor of trouble. It was worse than horse poo and twice as dangerous.

With trouble this big, there was only one person in Liberty tough enough to beat it back.

Theodora Hendricks deposited her buckskin satchel on The Second Chance Grill's counter and commenced to enjoy her favorite pastime—staring down Ethel Lynn Percible until the old fool, darting between tables like a drunken firefly, dropped a platter of dishes.

The crash of china and Ethel Lynn's high-pitched squeal threw the dining room into silence. A tot at table seven shaped his mouth into an *O.* At table nine a group of businessmen stopped to stare mid-chew. But everyone in town was used to the decades-long feud, a state of war that broke out daily. Diners quickly returned to their meals.

Ethel Lynn scooped the broken dishes onto her tray and returned to the counter. "Theodora, you're a boil on the butt of humanity," she said by way of greeting.

"Thank you for noticing." Theodora stuck her corncob pipe into her mouth.

"Why don't you find a child to terrorize? I'm thirty minutes from the end of my shift and in no mood for the likes of you." Ethel Lynn dumped the broken dishes into the garbage.

"Time has taken your beauty but rest assured it's left you stupid. I'm here for dinner. I need a menu."

"What you need is a swift kick in the behind."

"And you're the one to give it?"

"Not if you're carrying your Saturday Night Special." Ethel Lynn gave the buckskin satchel the once-over. "Are you armed and dangerous?"

"None of your beeswax."

"Oh, why don't you go and shoot a squirrel? I was in perfectly fine spirits until you arrived." Ethel Lynn smoothed down the lacey collar of her vintage dress. "Would you like to hear tonight's specials? We have a nice beef stew I'm happy to season with arsenic."

"Keep it up, missy. Wear down the last thread of my patience, and I will use my gun." Theodora settled her bony elbows on the counter. "Where's my coffee?"

A steaming cup appeared beneath her nose. She'd just taken a sip and fished a match from her satchel when someone said, "Mrs. Hendricks, please don't light your pipe. Smoking makes me want to puke."

The interruption lifted what was left of Theodora's brows.

Swiveling, she discovered young Snoops Keeley sliding onto a barstool. The girl's purple spectacles were dotted with raindrops from the April storm passing through Liberty. In fact the child was soaking wet, her dark hair a windblown mess and her eyes darting faster than Ethel Lynn when she was in one of her more jittery moods.

The child's distress brought Ethel Lynn forward. "Snoops, you look tuckered out! Did you bicycle here in the rain? What if you'd been struck by lightning?"

"I had to come." The girl turned to Theodora. "Mrs. Hendricks, I need to talk to you."

"Should I send the waitress away so we can chat in private? Mind you, she's got mostly fizz between her ears. She probably can't follow along anyway."

The insult drew Ethel Lynn's head back. "Put a lid on it. Can't you see the child's upset?" She took Snoops by the hand. "Go on, dear. What's the matter?"

The gentle prodding spilled a story from Snoops so worrisome that Theodora listened with her heart trembling like a sparrow with broken wings.

Naturally the girl had no idea why anyone would break into the computer network of the *Liberty Post.* She didn't understand why anyone would target Birdie in particular. But Theodora knew. Damn it all to hell and back—she knew.

Finishing, Snoops swiped a lock of wet hair from her cheek. "I didn't think I should call Birdie and Hugh. They're still out on an interview."

They'd reluctantly gone to Bell Corners to cover the quilting contest held by the Daisy Lane Women's Club. It took a spirited argument then threats to get their butts in gear, but they'd finally obeyed Theodora's command. She didn't give a rat's ass if Hugh preferred reporting on dirty politics and corporate corruption. Common folk also deserved news coverage.

Theodora eased her lined face into what she hoped was a look of compassion. "Don't worry. I'll tell them about the hacker," she assured the girl. She was better versed in expressions of irritation or rage, but didn't wish to frighten Snoops.

"Mrs. Hendricks, why is someone hacking the newspaper and messing around with Birdie's bank account?"

The question was right on the money—literally.

Stalling for time, Theodora stirred cream into her coffee. Anxiety rose like lightning up her spine, but she donned a poker face and sorted her thoughts. She'd loved Birdie, her lost kin, ever since the sassy pickpocket had arrived in town last year with a streak of goodness so deep, it was no surprise she'd turned her life around.

Unfortunately she was also the child of no-good Wish Kaminsky—one of the most nefarious swindlers ever to work the continental United States. Wish was a master of disguise and craftier than a fox. For years the Feds had been tracking her whereabouts. They'd never taken her into custody.

Snoops leaned close. "Mrs. Hendricks? Why is someone after Birdie?"

"To punish her." Theodora shook her head with disgust. "There's one person who doesn't take kindly to Birdie coming out on top. Lord knows jealousy brings out the worst in some people. Of course, some people so bad they don't need to stir their most poisonous emotions. They're just plain evil to begin with."

A breath stuttered from Ethel Lynn. "Heavens! You don't mean .. ?"

"I surely do. Hellfire and damnation—we can't let Wish get anywhere near our Birdie."

"Who's Wish?" Snoops asked.

Perspiration beaded on Ethel Lynn's forehead.

"Where are my smelling salts? I feel faint."

"Go ahead and drop, old fool. I'm not catching you." To Snoops, Theodora said, "Wish Kaminsky is the worst type of criminal, a black-hearted woman who'll cause nothing but harm to Birdie *and* our fine town." She paused for a perilous moment. "She's Birdie's mother."

At the explanation, Snoops paled. "Yikes. Who'd want a mother like that?"

Theodora harrumphed. "No one with an ounce of common sense." Years ago Wish had scammed one of Liberty's leading citizens out of hundreds of thousands of dollars, not that the sorry tale was something to share with a junior high student. "For all we know, she's already on her way here. When she arrives, she'll cause nothing but financial ruin to any citizen unlucky enough to cross her path."

"You mean she won't just hurt Birdie? She'll come after the whole town?"

"She's greedy to the core. It'll start with Birdie but won't end there. She likes nothing better than scamming good people."

"We should tell the police. They'll stop her."

"They'll try. It won't work. Wish has been evading capture all her life."

"But we have to do something." Snoops looked from one woman to the other. "We'll think of something, right? Mrs. Hendricks, you won't let anything bad happen to Liberty, will you?"

"Of course not. What we need is a way to find Wish before she causes trouble. I don't mind saying it'll be difficult. Once she cleaned out the savings of an entire retirement community in a matter of days. She was dressed like a man from a phony investment firm and fooled them all."

Ethel Lynn lowered her voice to a conspiratorial tone. "I heard she bilked thousands from a pension fund in

Denver. Wish disguised herself as a businesswoman from a local bank. Had everyone fooled. Hugh has all the details. Oh, this is awful!"

Snoops' eyes rounded. "So we won't know who we're looking for? That's not good."

Ethel Lynn patted the moisture from her brow. "We'll need to follow every newcomer to Liberty, every stranger stopping by The Second Chance Grill or staying in town. Heaven above, how will we prevail? Liberty is growing fast—there's the new housing development going up on the east side of town. It's not like the old days when we knew everyone who lived here."

Considering, Theodora finished her coffee. After a moment, she said, "Bounty hunters."

Only seasoned professionals, ex-cops and steely detectives with a hound dog's ability to stalk prey, had a chance of apprehending a grifter as slippery as Wish. Hopefully they'd bring her down before she got within spitting distance Liberty.

"How do we hire bounty hunters?" Ethel Lynn asked. "Through the local police?"

"We'll start there." Thanks to her connections, Theodora knew the state police would help too. "I have faith in our men in blue, but we need more than they'll provide. We need to bring in enough hunters to cover the whole U.S. of A. There's no telling where Wish is hiding—best if we stop her before she crosses the Ohio state line."

"What are you saying? We need lots of people to look for her?"

"We need every able body we can get. And a sizeable bounty for the man who brings her to justice."

Breaking her silence, Snoops said, "Let's use social media. We'll set up websites like we did when Blossom was sick. If you're offering a big reward, we'll get results fast."

The offer warmed Theodora. "I think you're on to something," she said, glad for the girl's quick thinking.

"I can take care of everything you need." Snoops removed her laptop from her backpack and set it on the counter. "What should the post say?"

Mulling it over, Theodora waved her cup through the air. After the sweet brew arrived, she dug a pad and a pen from her satchel and wrote swiftly, crossing words out and starting again. Finally she looked up with satisfaction.

"I'll take care of the reward." She slid the page forward. "Post this far and wide. Add my email at the bottom. I'll ask Hugh to help me sort through the responses. We'll find some good men."

"And women," Ethel Lynn put in. "There's no telling who will go hunting for Wish." She thought of something else. "Should we mention this to Birdie?"

The query put a frown on Theodora's lips. "I sure don't have a hankering to scare her half to death. She's talking marriage with Hugh, and enjoying the first decent spell she's had in her life. Let me think on it."

Snoops drew her finger across her mouth. "My lips are sealed unless you decide to tell Birdie." Scanning the words Theodora had written, she added, "Wow. This is good stuff."

Quickly the girl typed:

WANTED
DEAD OR HOG-TIED
The no-good con woman and mistress of disguise
Wish Postell Kaminsky
$100,000 Reward

Chapter 2

Dabbing her forehead with a napkin, Wish Kaminsky nodded to the bartender. "More Tequila."

The tavern, as lean and long as a bowling alley, swam in shadow. With afternoon waning, most of the patrons were paying their bills and wandering back into the treacherous heat. Above the grimy bar the fans stood motionless.

On her laptop, the Wanted post by Theodora Hendricks flickered.

Damn the old hag. They'd never met, although Wish knew they were distantly related. Second cousins or third, it didn't matter. What *did* matter was the reward Theodora offered, a prize large enough to build a troop of bounty hunters determined to find their quarry.

Yesterday Wish had stumbled across the announcement during her daily Google search. She enjoyed reading old news clips about her exploits in the Pacific Northwest, where a mysterious woman had scammed a dozen men. She relished the articles from Miami about how she'd cleaned out the life savings of half the retirees in an assisted living community. The self-congratulatory high fizzled when she came across the electronic version of a

Wanted poster that sported a dozen photos of her in various disguises.

Dismissing the memory, she canvassed the bar. A few men were finishing their beers; none glanced her way. She was dressed like one of them, just another *hombre* in Mexico City.

Were bounty hunters massing on the other side of the Rio Grande? They might begin the hunt in Texas where she was last spotted after a scam in Dallas. All those retired Americans, willing to dole out cash for drugs they believed would allow them to live forever—*why* were people so stupid? She'd racked up thousands before the authorities caught wind of the deal. Luckily a tip from one of her lovers had provided enough time to board the flight to Mexico City.

And, prior to discovering Theodora's notice, she'd already booked her next trip to the States. What she hadn't expected was Theodora's bounty hunters gumming up the works.

No matter. They wouldn't make her deviate from the plans she'd spent months devising. The simplicity of this latest scheme was equaled only by its cunning, a perfect combination of diversion and tactic designed to wreak the most damage. Thanks to Theodora's meddling, the prize was now harder to reach. Not impossible, just harder, and the complications merely focused Wish's determination.

The swarthy bartender placed the Tequila before her. Downing it, she let her eyes drift shut.

"Excuse me. Are you Rodriquez?"

A young man with a face pockmarked by acne materialized out of the bar's shadows. Next came his brother, who was just as thin. They looked like twin ferrets with their beady eyes and weak chins. Their hands were in constant motion, tripping up their faded jeans, brushing along their rumpled tee shirts. The shirts smelled like they hadn't been washed in a week. Ditching her revulsion, she nodded.

"I'm Rodriquez," she said, switching to the sensuous, feminine voice that drove men to their knees.

Registering surprise, the men stepped back in tandem. She grabbed the closer one by the wrist.

"Before we begin, there's one thing. If you ever steal from me, you'll regret it." She let him go and he scuttled back like a beetle caught in the light. "Are you as good as they say? You've come highly recommended."

"You bet I am," he said with thin bravado. His Adam's apple bobbed beneath his sallow skin. "We'd like to get out of Mexico, go home. If you've got a job that'll put us back in the States, we're taking it."

"I'm sick of this place," the second one said.

Beavis and Butthead, she thought, a couple of two-bit cons like so many she'd hired in the past: They were young, greedy, and as bright as a twenty-watt bulb.

They'd do.

"We'll start in Georgia," she said, "while I finish the plan." Sharing information about the bounty hunters sure to track their movements seemed unwise, and she added, "I'll need your services for a week. Two, tops."

The first one shrugged. "I like Georgia all right." Curiosity lit his dull gaze. "What's after that?"

Anticipation as thick as envy settled over Wish. The sweet taste of victory filled her mouth, a confection she'd season with stealth and rage. When she'd finished—when she'd won—she'd leave nothing but sorrow in her wake. As she always did.

"Ohio," she replied.

For the third day running, Theodora marched into the *Liberty Post* unannounced.

Finishing the article, Birdie tried to plaster on a

pleasant expression. Feeling anything but heartache was unimaginable now that Hugh had moved out. Amazingly the news hadn't been broadcast across town, at least not yet.

An impenetrable air surrounded Hugh when he arrived each morning for work. He remained cordial, but it was clear he wasn't ready for a discussion; which made finding a way to repair their relationship impossible. Would he soon ask for the engagement ring back? With nervous movements Birdie twirled the one-carat solitaire on her finger as Theodora approached.

For a woman past her eightieth birthday Theodora took the center aisle at a fast clip, her gaze gleaming with approval as she surveyed her surroundings. The newsroom was still coming together, the desks neatly arranged in two rows and some of the hardware—computers, printers and scanners—still in boxes.

Snoops and Blossom had marked out territory in the second row, giving their desks an adolescent air with mason jars brimming with colorful markers and a candy jar filled with a variety of sweets. Both girls were too young to officially hold a job at the *Liberty Post*. They certainly didn't have scheduled hours. But their contribution, after school and when they wandered in during the weekends, was welcome. The girls' parents had assured Birdie and Hugh that payment out of petty cash was fine for a couple of twelve year olds.

Snoops peered around the side of her iMac. "Hi, Mrs. Hendricks." The girl fiddled with her eyeglasses. "Do you have time to, uh, look at my story?"

"Happy to." With barely a nod in Birdie's direction, Theodora brushed on past.

Birdie spun around in her chair. "Snoops, you don't write articles for the paper. You handle tech."

"I'm practicing, okay? Someday I *will* have an article worth publishing."

Theodora stood behind the chair as Snoops typed madly, her fingers lifting only to snatch a chocolate from the small pile she'd heaped beside the keyboard. Yesterday had been the same, with Theodora appearing in the afternoon and showing an interest in the girl's stabs at composition.

Since when did Theodora dole out lessons in copywriting?

Usually she stuck to nagging Birdie or Hugh about covering some impossibly dull local event like the church social or the latest gossip at the 4-H Club. The scuttlebutt was usually of earth-shattering importance, like Sam Smith's secret blend of feed for raising prize-winning hogs.

Blossom hopped out of her chair and went to Snoops' desk. She murmured in Theodora's ear, her hands slicing the air. A prickly sensation darted up Birdie's neck.

"Okay, what's going on?" she asked Theodora. "I get the feeling you're leaving me in the dark about something."

Theodora jauntily adjusted her felt hat, the silk roses bouncing. Today she'd paired up a vintage herringbone jacket with a flowery skirt and ankle boots of black leather. She looked like a cross between Sherlock Holmes and a biker chick.

"Secrets?" Her eyes flashed. "You think we're the ones keeping secrets?"

She probably meant the tiff with Hugh, a topic they would *not* discuss if Birdie had her way. "Don't change the subject. You've stopped by three days in a row. It's not because you miss my company. You're never this sociable."

"Don't sass me." Theodora peered at the stairwell leading to the second floor. "Is Hugh upstairs? Taking a nap?"

"He doesn't nap." Not that she knew for certain. Maybe he was out drinking every night and catching a few Z's in the afternoons at the Perinis' house. A single guy, all over again.

31

"Is he out on an interview?"

"I don't know, Theodora." Tracking his whereabouts was impossible now that they were barely speaking. "If I had to guess, he's probably out on a story. He lives for ink."

"Cut the crap. You know what I'm really asking. Has he moved out?"

"I'm sharing that information on a need-to-know basis. You don't need to know."

"Yes, I do. I've been looking at invitations and whatnots—thought I'd host a wedding this summer, something nice in Liberty Square. If he's flown the coop, you might as well spit it out before I waste too much money."

The announcement caught Birdie off-guard. Theodora had planned to host the wedding? The generous offer was totally unexpected.

The prospect dampened Birdie's already low mood. It was just like Theodora to fling impatient questions then follow up with the sweetest generosity. Not that her kindness would amount to much. Eyes downcast, Birdie ran her finger around the diamond sparkling on her finger with heaven-sent promise. She didn't deserve something so beautiful, not after the way she'd treated Hugh. In fact she didn't deserve Hugh, a man who'd waited for her to set aside the bad habits she'd learned as a child in a family of swindlers. Maybe she shouldn't wait for him to ask for the ring back. Should she return it with a heartfelt apology for taking everything he'd offered for granted?

Blossom wandered up. "Mrs. Hendricks, give Birdie a break." The girl rested a hand on Birdie's shoulder in a touching demonstration of solidarity. "Can't you see you're upsetting her?"

"It's all right, kiddo," Birdie murmured. She gave Blossom a quick hug. To Theodora, she said, "Hugh is staying at Blossom's house. Anthony offered a guest bedroom. I don't know how long Hugh plans to stay at the Perinis'. Needless to say, I don't think I'll hear wedding bells anytime soon."

"He moved out or you threw him out? The way you two fight, anything is possible."

"I didn't want him to go."

She'd been stunned by his decision. Her inability to see how unhappy he'd become probably meant she was dumb *and* ungrateful. In retrospect, it was amazing he'd considered marrying her at all.

"Wipe your tears away, Birdie. He'll be back," Theodora said. For a long moment she wrapped herself in a brooding silence. She appeared to come to a decision, her mouth working as she mumbled incomprehensible words. At last she added, "He won't stay at the Perinis'. He knows you need protection. This afternoon he went to talk to the police. If you haven't seen him, I'm guessing he's still there."

Something worrisome swirled through the air, a portent of bad news. The hairs on the back of Birdie's neck bristled. "He's interviewing someone at the police department? About what?"

"Not an interview—he's getting their advice on how to protect you if your mother comes to town." Reconsidering, Theodora added, *"When* she comes to town."

All thought evaporated from Birdie's head. Then her mind rushed forward with a tumult of emotion.

No, it wasn't possible. Her mother wouldn't risk coming here.

Years ago she'd made powerful enemies in Liberty after she'd swindled retired banker Landon Williams out of several hundred thousand dollars. Everyone within a fifty-mile radius knew the story of how Landon had been broken by his love for the conniving woman who simply vanished one day. No one would roll out a welcome mat if

Wish were foolish enough to return. Except the police, with handcuffs at the ready.

Throughout Birdie's childhood, her mother had neglected to reveal that Landon was her biological father. In the last six months, he'd become a cherished part of Birdie's life; a sweet-spoken man who offered quiet counsel on how to grow the *Liberty Post* when he wasn't plying her with lavish dinners at his mansion near Lake Erie. She dreaded the thought of how the news of her mother's reappearance might increase the depression that had stalked him for years.

There was a bigger problem. Last year Wish had sent Birdie to Liberty with the clue passed down in their family for generations, *Liberty safeguards the cherished heart.* At the time, they hadn't known if the stories were true.

Supposedly their ancestor Lucas Postell had sent the freedwoman he'd loved from Charleston, South Carolina to an unknown northern state to live until The Civil War ended and he could rejoin her. Birdie had not only discovered that Justice Postell had carried two bags of rubies on her journey north. She'd also found Justice's descendants—Theodora and the Hendricks clan. Birdie was now as close to them as she was to Landon. She'd do everything in her power to protect them.

Her heartbeat quickening, she began pacing before her desk. "My mother heard about the rubies. On the Internet, in a news story—somehow she knows. She'll want the gems, and a way to punish me in the bargain."

Theodora went to her. "There's no sense in working yourself up into a panic. If she steps one foot in Liberty, we'll be waiting."

"Hugh is asking law enforcement for help?"

"He's filling them in. The State Troopers put out an APB. Our local boys are also on the lookout. You needn't fret. Everything that can be done is being done."

The news made her unaccountably cold. "What makes you think my mother is coming here?" She rubbed her arms with brisk movements.

"What a foolish question! We've caught her red-handed. She's been poking around in the *Liberty Post's* computers like a nasty dog. Snoops says she hacked the system."

The explanation didn't make sense. "My mother is clueless when it comes to computers. She's better at the traditional con, like bilking seniors out of their retirement funds or taking advantage of rich, lonely men."

Snoops piped up. "She's the best hacker I've ever seen. If she isn't the one messing around in our files then she hired someone really good."

"She doesn't trust anyone. I can't imagine she'd hire a computer hacker to take the lead on a job."

Usually her mother hired stooges for small roles in a con but never for something this big. She was suspicious and greedy, incapable of sharing something as valuable as the rubies she evidently planned to steal. If that was her real goal.

Theodora rubbed her chin. "What makes you sure Wish can't hack a computer?"

"She never learned how to use the simplest programs or navigate the Internet. She hates computers."

"And you believed her? Lord above. Wish Kaminsky wouldn't think twice about lying to her own child. By my reckoning, she purposely kept you in the dark."

Birdie was still digesting the truth of the assessment when Hugh strolled in with the leather briefcase he stuffed full with his laptop, a tape recorder and other tools of the writing trade. He looked haggard, the dark patches beneath his eyes deeper than they'd been yesterday. Her heart lifted as he pivoted in her direction, her smile wide and welcoming. But her emotions sank as he caught himself and retreated. The urge to rush into his arms nearly sent her across the newsroom.

He stowed his briefcase beneath his desk. "So they've told you?" he asked her.

"About my mother? Yes."

"This morning a report came in from Atlanta PD. A woman fitting Wish's description used a fake credit card for a stay at a local hotel."

Birdie shrugged off the news. "Lots of women fit my mother's description." She wasn't yet prepared to believe her mother would follow her to Liberty, the only home she'd ever known. "We shouldn't jump to conclusions. Why do you think it was her?"

"The woman was dressed as a maid in the hotel. She pilfered half the rooms on the third floor, taking everything from jewelry to cash lying around. According to Atlanta PD, the heist took fifteen minutes or less."

Birdie bit her lower lip. "My mother *is* fast." Once during childhood, she'd watched her mother push her way into a crowd of women at a department store cosmetics counter. She'd made off with four hundred dollars in less than fifteen minutes.

Blossom wrinkled her nose. "What *does* Wish look like? I mean, when she's not wearing a disguise." She hugged her purse, a leather envelope of bright pink, to her chest. "Maybe I should camp out in my bedroom for a week or two. Who needs school when someone as scary as Birdie's mom is on the prowl?"

Hugh chuckled. "I think you're safe, kiddo. If you're wondering what Wish looks like, she could pass for Birdie's twin. Hard to tell she's twenty years older."

"She's big on protecting her assets," Birdie agreed. "I'll bet she still works out and schedules spa visits between scams."

"She's a consummate actress. Why wouldn't she take her ill-gotten gains and splurge at the spa?" Dropping the subject, Hugh approached Snoops. "Is there mail?" he asked her. "I have an hour to dig through it."

Snoops turned on her printer. "We got seven more responses this morning."

Another prickly sensation warned Birdie there was more they hadn't shared.

She'd had enough bad news for one day. At this very moment her mother was probably heading toward Liberty in a state of fury because a treasure had been found. But Birdie hadn't returned to her mother's side, and the prospect of losing out on something like a cool two million in rubies would make Wish intent on revenge at Birdie *and* the owner of the second bag of gems— Theodora.

"Let me have the names," Hugh was saying. The printer beside Snoops desk whirred then spit out his request.

Birdie snatched the page from his hand. "I'm officially at wit's end. Tell me *why* we're collecting names."

"I thought they got you up to speed." He gave Theodora an appraising glance.

A fiery impatience sizzled up Theodora's nearly five-foot frame. "Blast it all, Hugh—I didn't mention the bounty hunters. What, with you and Birdie on the outs and that demon of her mother sure to come to town, I thought we'd given her enough shocks for one day."

"You're hiring bounty hunters to track down my mother?" Birdie laughed shortly. "You're joking, right?"

Theodora shimmied her narrow shoulders. "We're going after big game, aren't we? Of course we need hunters." Mischief sparked her smile. "Welcome to my safari."

Chapter 3

Hector Levendakis stared down the barrel of the Glock and prayed for a quick death.

Who would've guessed he'd meet his end in the guise of a beautiful woman? Male pride edged past his fear. Better to have the Fates snatch him through a modern-day Aphrodite than some beast named The Hammer or Ice Man. A dying man's last glimpse of cleavage and pursed lips sure beat the alternative of clenched teeth and spittle.

Not that his fiancé was blowing kisses his way.

At the other end of the Glock she narrowed her gaze. When the gun bounced in her grip, his stomach plunged to the pavement.

Holy shit. He *was* going to die. Right here, right now, on an empty stretch of road in the Appalachian Mountains. So much for a weekend getaway of wine and roses.

Charlene lowered her chin and peered down the barrel. "Give me good news, Hector. Tell me you didn't lose all my money."

"Not all of it." He'd rescued some of her savings and a portion of the Two Musketeers' cash during one of the worst weeks of day trading ever. From the way Charlene planted her feet, the Glock gripped tightly, he doubted it mattered. He told her about what he'd salvaged then added, "I left five thousand in airline stocks. Leave it there. I'm betting you'll see a rebound before the month's out."

"You and your stupid bets," she sneered. "You're a no-good day trader who doesn't know when to buy or sell. Didn't I tell you it was too soon to move cash from the money market? And what about your stupid bet on the Spanish economy?"

"Hey! I figured a casino in Madrid was a no brainer."

She swiped at her bangs, jiggling the Glock and his guts. "I trusted you with the money I'd saved. You lost it. You need to die."

"No! Wait!" Flop sweat sprouted on his brow. "Baby, I'll recoup your losses, every cent."

"Liar." She released the gun's safety. The deadly *click* blurred his vision. "Say hello to my mama when you get to the other side. Tell her I miss her."

"I'm not going to hell." Charlene's mother had been a drinker and a shrew. "If you want to talk to your mama, send a telegram."

"How can you joke at a time like this?"

"Habit?"

Tears pooled in Charlene's limpid gaze. "Die, Hector."

Terror jellied his insides and he squeezed his eyes shut.

This was it. He hadn't even reached the age of thirty-five before Hades threw him into a boat on the river Styx. No kids to leave behind, no legacy, unless he factored in years of sequential and great sex with The Two Musketeers and then Charlene.

At least the Musketeers would cry at his funeral— well, Bunny would. Sil rarely succumbed to public displays of emotion even though her rectangular eyeglasses and buttoned up blouses hid a lounge singer struggling to emerge. She'd wear something sparkly to the viewing and throw herself across his coffin.

He'd just begun working on his petition for mercy from the Big Guy in the Sky when the squeal of tires snapped him to attention. The scent of burning rubber hit his nostrils and he pealed his eyes open. His teeth chattered in time with his fibrillating heart.

Sil's red Beemer, the "Just Divorced" present he'd given her years ago, veered to a stop within inches of Charlene's thighs. Catcalls and screaming, and Sil hurled a soda can at the woman with the weapon. Dodging incoming, Charlene leapt away from the bumper. Hitching up her thigh-hugging skirt, she rushed to the berm.

Admiration bloomed in Hector's chest. Man, his fiancée had gorgeous legs.

Inside the Beemer his two ex-wives wrestled seat belts and muffled tears. They were genuinely concerned for his safety, the angels. On the passenger side, Bunny hurled herself out with her amazing breasts bouncing.

She rounded on Charlene. "Are you crazy? He didn't lose your money on purpose!"

Charlene's lower lip wobbled. "I trusted him—we all did. He should've pulled everything out before the market turned."

"He'll make good on your losses." Bunny swung around, her strawberry blond hair whipping the air. "Won't you, Hector?"

"Sure, sweetums."

"We'll show you how and you'll listen to us. Right?"

"Whatever you say." He had no idea what she was talking about but a wise man knew when to play along.

Sil, as lean and dark as Bunny was plump and blonde, dashed across the deserted highway. She towered over Charlene in a threatening posture. "Give me the gun *now*."

The command snapped Charlene from her death-trance. Jerking her head to the side, she gulped down air. When she lowered the Glock, Sil rushed in to take possession.

Gingerly she deposited the gun in her purse. "Let's all calm down. Charlene, I want you to call my office next week for a session. Here's my card."

"I don't want your card. I want my money."

"We'll work on your wants later. What you *need* is more constructive strategies for handling aggression. We'll work on it together." Her features softening, Sil gave Hector the once-over. "Are you all right?"

"I'm fine, sugar pie." Psychologists. You had to love their sensitivity.

Feathery lashes batted affection his way. "If you say so."

But it was Bunny, a crack librarian who guarded the University of Virginia archives like a jealous Medusa, who surprised him.

Marching past the other women, she came toe-to-toe with his Peruvian loafers. Her cheeks were as red as Eve's apple, her green eyes spit fire, and he would've moved away if he weren't already pressed against the railing of the bridge. Hurtle down the embankment? Before their divorce, eighteen months of marriage revealed that Bunny's sweet personality hid a temper worth fearing. If he skimmed by with only a mashed ego and bruised pride he'd consider himself lucky.

He was still trying to work out if accidental suicide was a mortal sin when she slapped him across the face.

"What's the matter with you? Didn't I tell you to stay away from a yoga instructor with control issues?" She bounced her thumb at Charlene. "Tell the assassin the marriage is *off*."

"She *was* about to send me to Hades." Rubbing his jaw, which stung like the dickens, he turned to Charlene.

"Sorry, baby. We'd never make it as a couple." When she shrugged he said to Bunny, "Just out of curiosity, why do you care if I get hitched again?"

Bunny clamped her hands on her sumptuous hips. "Because you should be in love before you walk down the aisle." She whacked him on the chest. "Just because you're friends with a woman doesn't mean you should propose. Stop being so clingy."

"Hey!"

She poked him in the chest. "You're a good man but you're stupid. Fall in love, nitwit. *Then* get married." She regarded Sil. "Get it from the car, will you?"

Nodding, Sil sprinted away with Charlene following.

For the moment at least, Hector wasn't the main attraction.

The danger now past, his bones turned wobbly. His guts felt like pudding. Humiliated, he planted his feet in the choppy gravel. Men of the Levendakis tribe didn't show weakness in front of women—they were protectors, not sissies. If he dropped his ass on the pavement he'd nick his own pride.

The wind rolled down the mountainside and stirred the leaves on a thousand trees until a wild fluttering lifted on the air. Sunlight fell in golden beams that warmed his skin, if not his heart.

Charlene and the Two Musketeers weren't the only ones who'd watched their money evaporate in a bad spell of day trading.

Hector had staked his entire savings on established stocks and new ventures alike, certain the wealth bubbling up in the ever-expanding market would end his money woes for good. Five years from forty, he was starting over with nary a cent to his name.

Were the Fates done throwing roadblocks in his path?

The answer was an unequivocal 'no' when Sil returned from the car waving a sheet of paper. More bad news? He tried to firm up the pudding in his guts as she handed the sheet over.

He read quickly. A fierce looking old woman in Liberty, Ohio was offering six figures for the apprehension of a swindler named Wish Kaminsky. Dragging his hand through the curls carpeting his skull, Hector grunted.

"I'm not a bounty hunter." He shoved the page at Bunny. "I'm an investment counselor."

Sil, who'd pulled Charlene into a motherly embrace, rolled her eyes. "And you're a traveling salesman, a scuba instructor, a weight loss guru . . . remember the pyramid scheme with Acai juice? How much did you lose on that plum, Hector?"

"You got your investment back!"

"Yes, you always protect the women even if you go down in flames." She grinned. "Your chauvinism does have its perks. Now you need to recoup our nest eggs once again."

Bunny hopped up and down. "You can do it, Hector! You can do anything you set your mind to."

"For at least ten minutes," Charlene added. She colored. "I'm not talking about sex. You drift from job to job but in some respects you have more than your share of staying power."

"Yeah, yeah, yeah." Hector snatched the page back, drawing a squeak from Bunny.

WANTED
DEAD OR HOG-TIED
The no-good con woman and mistress of disguise
Wish Postell Kaminsky
$100,000 Reward

Liberty, Ohio. Just his luck. He had a great-aunt in

44

Youngstown and a herd of cousins in Akron. The Levendakis clan bred like rats and roamed like locusts. While he'd grown up in Philly most of the tribe oozed Greek culture all the way to the Indiana border. Clannish and superstitious, some of his relatives kept goats for the milk while others spit on the kids to protect them from evil spirits. They were all pushy and loud. Would a jaunt to Ohio mean he'd have to look any of them up? Dread climbed his spine and he shivered.

If he nabbed this Wish character quickly he could get the reward and get out.

Besides, apprehending a woman was easy. He'd been taking down the weaker sex since he'd first caught the love bug at the ripe old age of twelve. His problem was keeping one once he'd bagged her. Not that he had designs on romancing a grifter nearly twice his age even if she did look thirty years old in the nun's photo Bunny showed him. How did Wish Kaminsky do it? He might not admire her chosen profession as a con artist but she was incredibly attractive in many of the photos. But he could do without the convenience store surveillance photo of her dressed like a man.

So he'd be a bounty hunter for a week or two. No doubt Sil and Bunny had already packed his RV for the long road ahead.

The sweethearts.

Chapter 4

Drowsy from the all-nighter behind the wheel of his RV, Hector pulled into Liberty right before lunchtime.

The town square looked peaceful and pretty. Yellow daffodils framed the three-story brick courthouse at the north end of a center green dotted with maple trees and bisected neatly by a cobblestone walk.

At the other end of the green, a sugar shack he bet was still used to boil maple syrup sat nestled in shade. The shops surrounding the Square looked prosperous with customers visible behind large picture windows or standing outside storefronts enjoying the April breeze.

Banks of tulips waved from flower boxes that reminded him of long-ago childhood trips in Philly with his late mother, the hours-long journey from one greenhouse to the next during her finicky pursuit of the perfect bedding plants. If she were still alive, she would've approved of his visit to a town like Liberty. She'd dreamed of escaping Philly's blustering noise and crowded streets for a more pastoral lifestyle.

Slowing the RV, he double-checked the address for the interview. He'd expected to meet the mysterious Theodora Hendricks at a law office or even the local police department, but no—it seemed they'd meet at the only restaurant within sight, a quaint eatery called The Second Chance Grill.

Interviewing potential bounty hunters in a restaurant seemed odd, but what did he know? Hector parked the RV and went inside.

The place was jammed with diners at every table and down the long counter in back near the kitchen. A gum-chewing waitress darted between tables. He paused to take in the patriotic decorations festooned throughout the dining room, an extravaganza of pewter sconces set aside bucolic paintings of Colonial America, and gilt-framed portraits of George Washington and other historical personages. The Persian rugs flung out upon the gleaming oak floors and the picture window dressed in deep folds of patriotic bunting lent a welcoming air.

At the counter, a woman was dressed in 1960s era clothes. She splashed coffee in the general direction of the cups lined up before her customers.

"Excuse me." Hector tried not to stare at her get-up, a satin cocktail dress that brought back childhood memories of loud Greek aunts huddled around the Canasta table. "I'm looking for Theodora Hendricks. I have an interview."

"You're Hector?" When he nodded, she offered a hand feathered with veins and sporting bright pink nail polish. "I'm Ethel Lynn Percible. Good heavens, you're a handsome rascal. Married?"

"Not today." If this was feminine interest, the vamp was aiming for the wrong man. She was as old as his bossy Nana, minus half the body mass.

Evidently she read his discomfort as bashfulness. "Now, don't be shy. You should be honored—Theodora dismissed most of the applicants. She chased one man out with her rifle. He was in tears."

"No kidding." If the vamp was serious about the

rifle, maybe he should get back in the RV. He'd seen enough gunplay for one week.

"Theodora is particular about what she's looking for."

"Where is she?"

"Back there."

He followed Ethel Lynn's gaze over the diners' bobbing heads to a table in the corner. Someone had cordoned off the area with the kind of heavy gold cord used in swanky bars to keep out the riffraff.

Inside the enclosure, a petite crone caught Hector's attention with a glittering stare. She wore a severe navy suit with epaulets on the shoulders and a hunting cap in camouflage green. The Winchester rifle resting on the wall behind her seemed to highlight the air of hostility drifting like fog in his general direction.

The man beside her looked friendly enough—he was tall, dark and almost as handsome as Hector—but the raisin-skinned general to his right? Theodora Hendricks looked capable of leading soldiers in the nastiest sort of guerrilla warfare.

Second thoughts nearly propelled him outside. "Am I the only applicant?" he asked Ethel Lynn. He was no coward, but hiding in a crowd sounded better.

"There's no one else. Don't keep Theodora waiting. She doesn't have much in the way of patience."

"Right." Taking the plunge, he weaved his way to the corner.

When he reached the rope, Theodora held up her hand. "You're Hector Levendakis from Philadelphia?"

"Yes, ma'am." He wondered if a salute was in order.

"You're late."

"Only by twenty minutes. It's a long drive from Philly."

A dissatisfied grunt burst from her lips. "Do I look like I care?"

"Not really."

She shuffled papers. "We received two letters of recommendation, both from ex-wives. They say you're reliable, all evidence to the contrary." She held him in a disapproving stare. "It's not often a man breaks a woman's heart and she wants him anything but dead."

"I recently broke my engagement to a woman planning to send me to Hades. She's not supportive like my ex-wives. Does that count?" He lifted the rope then let it swing free. "May I enter? It's easier to chat about murderous women face-to-face."

She appeared to weigh his request with misgiving and a peculiar distaste, as if his inquiry was so repugnant it turned her stomach. Or maybe she just had indigestion. Given her advanced years, anything was possible.

Finally she waved him inside. "You may enter." She motioned him into a seat then made introductions. After he shook Hugh Schaeffer's hand, she asked, "You were in the military before hanging out your shingle as an investment counselor?"

"Actually it was a few years back. Two tours in Iraq." It seemed wise not to mention the career disasters endured since then, a humiliating string of missteps culminating in his demise as a day trader. "I've been looking for a change, something to get me out from behind a desk."

"You don't say."

Hugh, taking notes until now, began tapping his pen on the table. "Do you have a permit to carry a gun?" He looked like he'd pulled all-nighters for a week straight, and Hector sensed the guy's involvement in the capture of Wish Kaminsky was somehow personal. "Not that we want you to use it. Wish is a con artist but she's never been involved in crimes of violence. You may need a gun to corner her until the police arrive to take her into custody."

"I can do that. I have a permit, and enough sense

not to pull the trigger." He'd stashed his Glock, the one his ex-fiancé had wielded, in the RV. Hector thought of something else. "How many bounty hunters have you hired?"

Theodora's brow wrinkled like worn paper. "Counting you? Seven. Five out of state and the sixth covering Ohio's southern counties. You're responsible for Liberty, assuming Wish gets this far. We're hoping she won't."

"Only seven? With a reward this large, I'd expect more applicants."

"Lord, we've had those. Mostly ne'er do-wells and irresponsible fools. Even saw a tattoo artist who'd driven all night from Nashville. Big as a Sumo wrestler and as sharp as a marble."

"I hope he didn't make the list."

"He didn't. Those that did are professional bail enforcement agents. Figured I'd add you to the stew because you're a jack-of-all-trades and flighty like the no-good mistress of disguise we're aiming to apprehend. I'm not holding my breath, but you might get a bead on Wish faster than the rest of us. Stranger things have happened."

The remark about being flighty wasn't nice, but he took it in stride. "Your confidence is reassuring."

"In your dreams." Theodora screwed down her hunting cap, her eyes mere slits. "It's a stretch, but I'm assuming you've got brains in your head. You'll have to do your homework for any chance of success. Wish's cons run from simple thefts to elaborate financial schemes. There's no rhyme or reason to her methods. It's part of her charm."

"I'll do my best to find her." Not that the effort would matter. If he were placing a wager, he'd bet one of the professional bondsmen would take Wish down before she entered Ohio.

Hugh jumped in. "We're relying on local law enforcement for backup. The Feds are also looking for

Wish but if they're taking our concerns seriously, they aren't talking. It's understandable. Most of the leads they receive don't amount to much."

"You're convinced she's on her way here?"

"Positive."

Dredging up his military training, Hector mulled over a plan of attack. He was here, so he'd do what he could.

The first order of business? Check in with the local PD and glean the information they had on Wish. The material he'd received from his ex-wives didn't amount to much. Then it was off to the nearby bars and hotels, assuming Liberty had any—he'd dole out cash and his cell phone number in hopes someone would call in a tip. If Wish were a mistress of disguise, how to give bartenders and hotel maids an accurate description? He reflected on the printouts he'd left in the RV of Wish in an impressive variety of guises. The only thing she couldn't hide was her height, give or take a few inches for heels.

He was still sorting through the particulars of an impossible situation when, out on the street, a horn blared. Three teenagers jumped to the curb and a sweet, banana yellow Corvette glided to a halt before the restaurant.

The swing of glossy hair, and a stunning blonde got out. Long-legged with an angel's face complete with pouting lips, she had one of those pretty, upturned noses that Hector loved on a woman.

He did a double take. The woman entering The Second Chance Grill was Wish Kaminsky without one of her disguises.

His surprise elicited a sigh from Theodora's weathered lips. "Don't be a fool," she told him. "She isn't Wish. That's Birdie, her daughter."

The job of bounty hunter was sounding better all the time. "No one mentioned a daughter." Maybe he'd stick around for more than a few days.

"She owns our new daily with Hugh, the *Liberty Post.* I don't mind saying she's upset about the news of her mother heading our way."

"She needn't worry. I'll do everything I can to protect her."

Theodora grinned. "I just bet you will."

Hugh resumed tapping his pen, the pace of the incessant racket increasing as the blonde sashayed toward them, commanding the attention of every man in the dining room and producing dopey grins on the faces of two teenage boys lounging by the counter. Hector dug into his pockets for a breath mint.

Hugh's pen stopped tapping.

Beneath the table, a foot kicked at Hector's shin. On a yelp, he wheeled his attention.

Hugh leaned across the table. "Ground rules," he growled. "Birdie is off limits. You got that?"

"Mind telling me why?" Hector inched his chair back from the table.

"She's my fiancé."

Theodora grunted. "In theory. I haven't seen bluebirds circling your head or hers in days."

"Stay out of this, Theodora."

Hector rubbed his shin where Hugh had attacked him. "No bluebirds sounds like an opening to me," he said. "Especially if the birds have flown the roost."

A muddy sort of rage flashed across Hugh's face. But Hector was spared a volley of threats as Birdie let herself past the golden rope. She paused before the table in a cloud of alluring perfume, her attention leaping and assessing and, he was damn sure, sensing she'd just missed a pissing contest.

"Theodora, Hugh—I'll take it from here," she said, her matchless violet gaze landing on Hector. "Mr. Levendakis, why don't you come with me?"

"The room is ready for you, Birdie."

Officer Tim Corrigan ushered her down the corridor to the small, chilly room Birdie recalled all too well. Corrigan's broad shoulders nearly brushed the concrete block comprising the walls of a jail that still reminded her of a tomb. Tim and the other members of the Liberty police force were now her friends, a surprising state of affairs for an ex-thief.

Her past criminal activities, which culminated in the entire town learning she was a pickpocket after the story of her infamous family hit the papers, were largely forgotten. She was now viewed as a distant relation of the town's most respected citizen, Theodora, and the future bride of Liberty newcomer Hugh Schaeffer.

Thankfully no one knew she was on the outs with Hugh, and she wanted to keep it that way. Hopefully Hugh's decision to stay at the Perinis' for several days merely represented a complication in their relationship and not the demise of their plans to eventually marry.

Pulling from her musings, she paused as Hector jogged to catch up. Together they entered the room Officer Tim had set aside for their use.

The grey industrial table groaned beneath the stacks of folders the officer had set out for their perusal.

At random, Hector flipped open a folder. "These are crime reports on your mother. How did the Liberty PD come by all this stuff so quickly?"

"Theodora." The door softly clicked shut, leaving them to work. Taking a seat, Birdie added, "She called in favors across the U.S. for any and all information. There's probably stuff in the FBI archives we don't have in front of us, but not much."

Mirroring her movements Hector placed the reports in order by date. "You're saying that cranky old woman has connections from coast to coast? Hard to believe."

"Then here's another surprise. She's one of the wealthiest women in Ohio—old money, goes back generations. And don't call her cranky. We're related."

He produced a look of disbelief so pure, she nearly laughed.

Hector really was too handsome with the tousled curls scattered across his brow. His limpid brown eyes, framed thickly with lashes, danced across her face in search of an exaggeration regarding her blood tie to Theodora.

She'd already grown to like his fizzy personality and expansive gestures, the way he stayed in constant motion. Even now he sifted through the folders quickly, gleaning dates on crime reports as his foot tapped an uneven melody beneath the table. Sure, he spent too much time casting sidelong glances at her breasts. But she sensed the high-strung man before her was as trustworthy as Hugh.

The tapping stopped long enough for him to ask, "How is a tall drink of a woman like you related to a petite black woman who looks like she's a member of the NRA? No offense, but I don't see the family resemblance."

"Oh, it's there. One of my ancestors from South Carolina owned a plantation. His name was Lucas Postell."

"He owned a plantation? Like *Gone With the Wind?* Chicks in too much clothing and gents with lots of cash?"

"Basically. After his wife died, he fell in love with a beautiful slave. He sent her north as a freedwoman."

"You mean he sent her north with the rubies used for collateral to start your newspaper." When she looked up, impressed with his knowledge, he added, "I did the Google thing on my phone after you came into The Second Chance Grill. I didn't get to the part about you being related to Theodora, not with your boyfriend attacking me."

"Hugh attacked you?"

"He's a kicker. Want to see the bruises?" Hector rolled up the leg of his beautifully tailored pants. He was clearly pleased with the prospect of showing off skin.

She chuckled as he swung his leg closer. "Save the peep show. I believe you." Hector Levendakis might be a lot of things but he wasn't modest. "By the way, Hugh isn't my boyfriend. We're engaged."

"Theodora made it sound like marriage isn't a sure thing. If you need someone to talk you out of it, I'm your man."

"Is that your idea of a come-on?"

"If it's working."

"It isn't."

"Don't give up on me." He rolled down the crisp navy fabric. "I have better pickup lines."

He puffed out his well-muscled chest, his expression endearingly boyish. Yet the way he absently fondled his right earlobe suggested that behind the bravado, he welcomed heavy doses of affection.

He'd returned to tapping his foot to whatever music bounced through his head and she thought, *Mama's boy*. But *his* mama had conjured a stunning specimen of manhood in the classic Greek style, all dark looks and hard physique. She'd just bet he was the pick of the litter.

It was impossible not to enjoy a man so flirtatious and amusing.

Of course, there was the added benefit of knowing she'd infuriated Hugh by waltzing out of the restaurant with Hector slavishly dogging her three-inch heels. If a little competition galvanized Hugh to move back in with her, where was the harm? She missed the culinary feasts he'd whip up and spooning against his slumbering form until daybreak. He never forgot to take out the garbage and knew his way around an ironing board and a laundry load of delicates. And he listened to her, encouraging her hopes and dreams when he wasn't criticizing her lousy money management skills or poor housekeeping. But he didn't hit her with complaints every day. At least he balanced the criticism with compliments about her natural newswriting abilities. Losing Hugh was like losing a wife.

She finished organizing the folders. In an attempt to draw Hector from his more salacious thoughts, she slid forward a recent photograph of her mother taken from a security camera at a gas station in Austin.

"It's blurry, but this is probably the best shot you'll find." With regret Birdie withdrew her hand from a photograph depicting her mother smiling pleasantly, her long mane of blonde hair tied loosely at the base of her neck.

"Will your officer pals make a copy? I'd like to keep this one with me."

"I'm sure they will."

Two notepads had been thoughtfully left on the desk. Hector pulled one close. "Okay, what do you think your mother plans to do once she gets to Liberty?"

The question lingered for an uncomfortable moment. "Punish me."

"Given her mercenary habits, it's not smart to get on her bad side. What did you do?"

Looking past Hector's shoulder, Birdie let the memories pull her out to sea.

"My ancestor, the plantation owner from South Carolina? I grew up hearing this story about how he gave something of great worth to the freedwoman he'd loved. At the beginning of The Civil War she brought it north with her."

"Yeah, the rubies. So what?"

"My mother spent years searching to find out if the story was true. The whole thing was hard to believe—the story was too far-fetched. But the idea that something valuable was hidden in a northern state, something precious . . . the idea ate at her like a disease. She hated the thought of missing out on some big treasure that originally belonged to our family. Which is how I arrived in Liberty last year—she sent me on the hunt."

"And the story *was* true."

"The rubies, the collateral used to open the *Liberty Post*—that's the treasure brought north by Theodora's ancestor, Justice Postell. Actually there are two bags of gems. Theodora owns the other."

"So your mother is peeved because she missed out on the goods?"

"Furious, I'm sure. You don't know her. If she's holding a grudge, she'll wipe out your bank accounts *and* ruin your best friend's reputation just for spite. I was supposed to report back to her, not fall in love with Hugh and make Liberty my home."

"Hey, it's okay. I won't let her near you."

Hector covered her fingers with his hand, pressing lightly to impart his heat to her chilled skin. He neared the slightest degree as if considering whether to draw her into a hug, his eyes lit softly and his mouth curving with gentle encouragement.

At the moment, sinking into the comfort he offered was a temptation.

Since learning of her mother's impending arrival, a black sickness had filled Birdie's gut, a sensation much worse than the usual anxiety she battled about good times ending and the bleak life she'd once known crushing the brief interlude of happiness she'd enjoyed in Liberty.

Slipping her hand out from under his, she reached for the list of arrest warrants the Liberty PD had compiled. "As you can see, my mother likes to prey on the elderly and lonely, single men. Not this time. I'm sure she'll first target me then branch out to hurt as many people as possible. It's just the way she is. We know she's been tampering with the newspaper. Snoops found someone had hacked into the system."

"Who's Snoops?"

"An eighth grader. Save your surprise—she's brilliant. Knows more about computers than anyone outside of MIT. She handles tech for the *Liberty Post*. Not the most complicated job in the world, seeing that we're just a start-up in a rural county."

"You have a *kid* handling systems?"

"You'll like her. She has a thing for the color purple and never goes anywhere without lugging food. If you're ever hungry, check her pockets. She's always packing munchies."

"Good to know." Hector scrawled a note on his pad before steering the conversation back to Wish. "So a hacker got into the newspaper. How do you know it's your mother?"

"She's been withdrawing small amounts from my checking, maybe as a scare tactic. I don't use the account and wasn't aware of the theft. If Snoops hadn't picked up on it, we'd still be in the dark."

"Nice tactic to scare you. Do you think she's putting you on notice?"

"About wanting the rubies?" A dry-throated laugh escaped Birdie's lips. The sickness filling her belly crept higher, wrapping tendrils of discomfort around her heart. "I'm sure you're correct. She knows I care about the people in this town. Maybe she'll threaten to harm my friends unless I hand over the rubies."

"Will you?"

She'd dodged considering the possibility.

Relinquishing the rubies meant the *Liberty Post* would go under. All the months of preparation would come to naught without the buffer provided by the collateral on the rubies, a stream of cash they needed until they were firmly in the black. With the newspaper's demise the dream she'd built with Hugh would evaporate just as quickly, the dream of building a respectable business—and a life—together. Hugh might then abandon her and return to his hometown of Akron, a possibility too unsettling to contemplate.

"Birdie, can I make a suggestion?"

She gave a stiff nod. "Sure. Anything."

Hector tossed over a handful of photographs of Wish in disguise, including a ballroom shot of a brunette in a silvery gown and another of a redhead in black silk and emeralds. The third photograph, of a jilted lover in New Orleans that Birdie vaguely recalled from her lonely childhood, depicted Wish hanging on his arm and beautifully turned out in a cashmere Chanel suit.

"Until we catch Wish, why not tone down your lifestyle?" He gave her haute couture the once-over, the lime green leather jacket and thigh-high floral skirt seemingly drawing less disapproval than the triple strand of pearls she'd looped around her neck. "Don't get me wrong—I'd put you on the cover of a fashion mag any day. But seeing the way you dress, it's like leaving a blood trail for a hungry wolf."

She smoothed her hand across the pearls then reached up to encircle her diamond earrings with nervous fingertips. The movement sent light sparkling across the walls of the interrogation room.

Of course his suggestion was sensible. After years of going without, she'd recklessly leapt into a pool of luxury. If Wish saw her riding high, she'd work even harder to bring Birdie down.

"And ditch the Vette," Hector was saying. "It's a dream ride but if I were your mother, it would be the first item in my grab bag. Can you stow it somewhere, find a rental? Something with dents and no curb appeal?"

"I'll see what I can do."

"Good deal." He started for the door. From over his shoulder, he sent a look of impatience. "Well, come on. I'd like a tour of Liberty's seediest bars and any hotels in the area. If anyone new stops by for a brewskie or a one-night stay, we need to know about it."

She followed him into the corridor. "Liberty doesn't have a hotel. There *is* a bed and breakfast. As for seedy bars, there's only one. It's right outside town."

"Let's start at the bar."

Murmuring her agreement, she smiled at Officer Corrigan as they walked through the front office. She felt better, in no small part because Hector's confidence gave hope. He'd formed a plan, which was better than waiting for her mother to strike. And there was still the possibility that one of the out-of-state bounty hunters would track Wish down before she reached Ohio—and Liberty. In the past she predictably went underground if one of her cons drew too much attention. Now she also had paid bounty hunters tracking her, a hard fact that provided some reassurance.

Midway across the reception area Hector stopped. She nearly careened into his back.

He raked his hand through his hair. "I guess this means the party has begun," he said.

There was nothing celebratory about his expression as he jogged through the reception area and into the parking lot. Birdie's scalp tightened with a premonition she couldn't dispel, a knowing that made her gait unsteady as she pushed through the door and into the harsh sunlight.

Gone from the parking lot was her sweet ride, the banana yellow Corvette.

Chapter 5

Wish took the country road hostage on a squeal of tires and a plume of burnt rubber.

Stealing the Vette was a lark made deliciously cruel after Birdie had stumbled into the police station's parking lot with a look of horror. The need to race to safety only afforded Wish a fleeting glimpse of her daughter. It was enough to assuage the bitterness grown thick in her blood.

Laughing, she glanced at her reflection in the mirror. She blew a kiss. *Mama's out for revenge.*

A self-congratulatory buzz sent warmth as heady as whiskey through her well-toned muscles and into cheeks that appeared disturbingly masculine beneath the fake mustache and beard she'd donned as part of her disguise. The fat suit she'd slipped her svelte frame into was itchy to say the least. But having gone undetected in Liberty for two days, she couldn't complain. The costume made her resemble a dozen nondescript and elderly men in Liberty, and she'd only worn the disguise in the afternoons when the local kids were released from school and shoppers were milling past the stores ringing Liberty Square. In the throng she hadn't received so much as a second glance.

Confident she'd evaded notice, she'd eavesdropped on conversations between those chattering adolescents, Blossom Perini and Snoops Keeley. Whether sitting in the center green slurping ice cream cones or wandering past the shops, the insufferable pair talked nonstop. The reconnaissance provided a bank vault of information about how Snoops protected the *Liberty Post's* computers from future hacks as well as the number of bounty hunters hired from the galling *Wanted* notice posted on the Internet.

Bringing her thoughts back to the present, Wish took a hairpin curve at 90 mph. With her free hand, she pulled open the glove box and dumped the contents on the passenger seat. A wad of bills rolled across the seat's supple leather. The greenbacks were banded together just like she'd taught Birdie when the girl had been nothing more than a twitchy child. The rest of the contents didn't deserve a close inspection—a sugary Valentine's Day card from her daughter's fiancé, a pack of mints and a hairbrush with a few strands of ash-blonde hair caught in the bristles.

At the intersection of Highway 6 and Glenn Corners, Wish veered the car onto the berm and came to a bumpy stop. Directly ahead the bluff swooped downward in an unfurled carpet of picturesque farms set against a blue sky unmarred by clouds.

Near the southernmost tip of the vista stood the barn housing Liberty's new daily. The place looked nearly deserted with only one car in the lot, an old Buick that Wish knew was owned by a stringer working part-time for the paper.

No doubt Birdie was still at the police station filling out the report about the theft of her car. The yellow Vette would quickly be discarded. And Hugh? He was probably still at the restaurant with the meddlesome crone who'd hired the bounty hunters—Theodora.

The survival instinct that had always served Wish drowsed beneath a more dangerous inquisitiveness.

Incapable of resisting the pull of curiosity, she steered the car back onto the road and drove toward the bright red barn, the infuriating symbol of everything Birdie had accomplished since arriving here.

How could six months in a ratty Ohio town change the daughter molded with harsh commands and judicious neglect, the keen pickpocket who'd drifted from state to state like the rest of her kin? There was a natural pecking order to life, to families, and the notion that Birdie now believed she was superior to the blood she'd inherited was unforgivable. It was like a slap in the face, a repudiation of the life Wish had built with cunning and deceit. Fire churned in her mind.

The Corvette crawled to a stop at the dusty road meandering toward the barn. Wish was fantasizing about burning the *Liberty Post* to the ground when a purple bicycle flashed by the Vette's hood. The girl was bicycling fast, sending puffs of dirt skyward. Her appearance surprised the woman who was rarely on the receiving end of a shock. In silent fury Wish gripped the steering wheel.

Why wasn't Snoops in school? The brat had caused enough trouble by detecting the hack of the *Post's* computers. Recently she'd built a firewall impossible to penetrate. It was an act of war.

On impulse Wish slid lower in the seat. Then she laughed when the girl, evidently worried Birdie had caught her playing the role of a truant, brought the bike to a halt about twenty paces off. She gave a slow, arching wave. When no response was forthcoming, the bicycle shot out of the lot and down the road in the direction from which it had arrived. More puffs of smoke rising from the road, and Wish's anger returned.

What was the harm in a quick game of cat and mouse? The child certainly deserved punishment for all the problems she'd caused.

Self-preservation and malice warred in Wish's

heart. Choosing malice, she followed the girl.

Sweat bloomed beneath Snoops' sweatshirt.

Now she was in trouble, real trouble, and Birdie was sure to give her an earful. Snoops pumped her legs, and the bicycle gained speed. She never should have impulsively veered off the path to the junior high and bicycled out to her job for a quick check of the firewall she'd built.

Skipping her morning classes was dumb but the substitute teacher in English wouldn't notice and ditching gym class, which followed, wouldn't hurt her GPA. Now she wanted to kick herself for not thinking the decision through.

Pedaling faster, she didn't dare turn around.

If she waited for the Corvette to catch up, what good would that do? Birdie would yell at her. There'd be a long speech about how school was important because you couldn't succeed in life without an education, *blah, blah, blah*. A waltz down memory lane would follow, something about the years Birdie wasted on less-than-admirable pursuits when she should've kept her butt in a chair at college, working toward a future that didn't involve snitching cash from purses or running from the law.

Good stuff, all of it, and Snoops sure didn't need the reminders. According to grown-ups like the school guidance counselor and her Algebra II teacher, Snoops was the junior high's smartest student. Usually she didn't make dumb choices.

But she was a member of Theodora's team of bounty hunters even if she'd never been anywhere near a gun *or* a criminal like Wish Kaminsky. The tech wizardry Snoops wielded was powerful ammo, and she'd wanted to check the firewall to ensure she was keeping Birdie's mom *out.*

Her heart played bongos as she took the next hill too fast. The bike skidded and she yelped. She managed not to lose her balance. Call it quits and face Birdie? The approaching hum of the Vette's engine probably meant the gig was up.

Unsure, Snoops glanced over her shoulder. What she saw tore the breath from her lips.

The car was gaining on her but Birdie wasn't behind the wheel. Snoops caught a glimpse of a man's beard and mustache beneath a cold stare.

Confusion turned to terror. He was *aiming right for her.*

"Heavens to Betsy! What have I missed?"

Ethel Lynn stumbled into the hospital room on tea-colored pumps much too fashionable for the sticks passing for her legs. The frippery dress she'd worn this morning to The Second Chance, a silk number with rosebuds on the bodice, had been replaced by her version of afternoon wear—a Jackie O-inspired hot pink suit. The fool had topped it off with a pillbox hat of the same abominable color and clunky bracelets that highlighted the liver spots on her wrists.

From her roost at the side of Snoops' bed, Theodora cast a withering glance. "This isn't a Broadway play, you old goat. There's nothing to see." She settled her hand on the side of the bed where Snoops, her right leg strung high in a cast, lay sleeping. "Why don't you go back to work? There are enough of us here. You aren't needed."

The impolite comment didn't produce the desired results. "Where are the dear child's parents?" Ethel Lynn, clearly intending to stay, approached the hospital bed.

"Home making dinner for the rest of their brood. They left after Snoops fell asleep. I promised I'd stay until they return."

Birdie was seated on the other side of the bed. "The Keeleys are such a nice family," she said, smoothing the blanket around Snoops' sleeping form. "They don't need this misery, and I'm responsible for it. How could my mother try to run a child off the road? How could she do something so reprehensible?"

Hector, standing behind her chair, gave her shoulder a reassuring squeeze. "I thought your mother never resorted to violence."

"This is a first. Usually her interests revolve around the next scam and an escape plan. She's as predictable as the flu."

"Aiming your car at a kid isn't normal behavior. If that trucker hadn't witnessed the accident, Snoops would still be lying in a ditch."

Anger simmered beneath the retort, alerting Theodora to something she'd missed.

Hector was doing his best to put a lid on his rage, rolling his shoulders and wiping his expression clean. She'd already decided he was a decent man who kept his animal instincts on a tight leash, a trick he'd undoubtedly learned during his years in the military. The sight of the injured child troubled him. He seemed incapable of observing Snoops for more than the most fleeting of moments before averting his eyes.

Did a deep sadness hide behind his sparkling personality, a regret so severe it had brought him to Liberty, of all places? If he'd deluded himself into believing he'd arrived merely to win the reward for Wish's capture, Theodora was sure he was mistaken. He'd come like a knight wounded from earlier battles, perhaps terrible battles. Yet he was determined to prevail.

"The trucker said the Corvette wasn't trying to hit Snoops," Birdie was saying, her voice high and strained. "From what he saw, she lost control and went flying."

Hector brushed off the defense. "C'mon, now. She

veered into the ditch because she thought Wish *would* hit her."

"Are you accusing my mother of intended murder? She's a lot of things—a lot of awful things—but she wouldn't kill anyone."

"Why are you defending her? With or without the bloodshed, she's a menace."

Theodora fisted her hands. "Enough with the debate!" Jangly tension put a sour tang in her mouth, the coppery taste of fear. And why not? Wish was as unpredictable as a rabid animal. "We don't know what Wish will do next. It's sensible to conclude she took aim because Snoops had locked down the *Post's* computers, barring another hack. If Wish *has* figured out Snoops is protecting the computers that means the no-good mistress of disguise has been in town for at least several days."

Ethel Lynn fell against the wall, her hat bouncing above feathery wisps of silver hair. "She's been here *for days?* We're doomed."

Hector favored Theodora with a look of incredulity. "Now, wait a second," he said. "You hired bounty hunters across the U.S. How did she slip into Ohio undetected?"

"They aren't miracle workers, son."

"At minimum, we should've received a warning."

"We did—just not in time."

"I didn't hear anything about it."

Theodora pulled up a text on her smartphone. She handed over the gadget. "Late this morning I got a message from a hunter in North Carolina. He'd heard about a pickpocket at a highway stop outside Columbus. The woman sounded like Wish. He was on his way to check out the lead when Wish ran Snoops off the road."

"You should've told me, Theodora. I need to stay in the loop."

"Who's running this three-ring circus, Hector—you or me? I was about to send you a text when I heard about

Snoops."

The heated exchange had grown loud. In the bed, the girl stirred. Her eyelids fluttered but Theodora knew she was deep under. The ordeal she'd endured had tuckered her out.

Bruises were blooming on the side of her face, the site of impact where she'd crashed to the ground, the garish yellow color seeping from her chin all the way to her temple. Her hands sported deep nicks where the doctors had removed bits of gravel from her tender skin, the wounds now covered by bandages. Surveying the damage, Theodora suffered a wave of anger so fierce she thought it might leave blisters in her throat.

Hector asked, "The bounty hunter from North Carolina—is he coming here?"

Theodora wrestled her emotions into silence. There'd be time later for rage. For now, she needed to keep her wits if they were to have any chance of catching Wish.

Ethel Lynn flitted close. "Theodora? Is he coming? We could use more help."

"He'll arrive soon. I've also sent word to three of the others. They're all coming."

"Do you think they'll find Birdie's new car? Such a shame if something so pretty is damaged."

Stifling a moan, Birdie scrubbed her face with her palms. "Knowing my mother, she'll total my car. Or torch it."

"Heavens!"

"Don't worry, Ethel Lynn. I can get another set of wheels." Birdie shot a glance at Hector, who smirked. "I've been thinking about trading down to a shabby ride. A dents-and-bents special."

Hugh strolled into the room. "Good plan," he said to Birdie. "Not that you have much choice. According to the Liberty PD, your car was totaled thirty minutes ago."

She covered her eyes then peered through her

fingers. "You're sure it's my car?"

"Oh, yeah. Banana yellow with a trail of fire. It went off a cliff near Lake Erie. Total smash-up. Check YouTube in a few hours—a boater got it on video."

"You sound pleased."

"About the boater watching the show? It probably made his day." Hugh withdrew a bag of peanuts from his pocket and tossed a few into his mouth. Chewing thoughtfully, he added, "Wish was nowhere in the vicinity. No surprise there. She's slipperier than a snake slithering in the rain."

"Unfortunately for me . . . and my car."

"Here's an idea. Get a Doberman to guard your fashion gear. Now that your mother has finished with the Vette, she's probably thinking about taking scissors to your Saks Fifth Avenue purchases."

"You and Hector should stop with the Vulcan mind meld regarding my taste in fashion. I get how my mother may be expressing . . . I don't know. Jealousy? Revenge because I'm doing all right without her? Oh, and thanks for the comedy routine, dear. It's just what I needed."

"More like what you deserve."

"Why don't I send *you* over a cliff, Hugh? Seeing that you didn't pack any compassion today."

"Whatever." His dismissive gaze left her and found Hector. "What are you doing here? Shouldn't you be working the streets?"

"I'm doing just fine where I am," Hector said with admirable composure.

"Because you're near my girl, you mean. News flash—I wasn't kidding when I said Birdie was off limits."

"I'm sure she can take care of herself. She doesn't need you marking her like a no fly zone."

"I *can* take care of myself." Birdie let hands fall to her lap. Then she flashed Hector a flirtatious look. "About your RV. Do you want to park it at my place? Plenty of room, and I'll feel safer with you nearby."

"Works for me. Skip the Doberman. I won't let Wish or her scissors anywhere near you."

Hugh's shoulders jerked as if he'd been zapped by stray electricity. "Hector isn't parking his love machine at our place. Have you *seen* the RV? It's got cheesy red curtains in the windows and a bumper sticker I can't repeat in polite company."

"Buddy, you're hitting below the belt. The curtains are a present from one of my ex-wives."

"Stop bickering!" Theodora stared the lot of them into silence. Hell and damnation, she wasn't going to watch the love birds trade insults any more than she planned to witness another pissing contest between Hugh and Hector. "We know Wish is in Liberty. She's making no secret how desperate she's become. Look at Snoops. The child has been hurt because a black-hearted thief has come to Liberty for reasons we have yet to discern. I want the three of you to stuff your hormones and put your heads together. We have to figure this out."

Mention of Snoops' injuries doused the competitive air swirling through the hospital room. Eyes lowered, Hugh nudged Hector out from behind Birdie's chair and narrowed his eyes in the predictable way that indicated he was turning something over in his brain. He was one of the finest investigative journalists in Ohio. Surely he'd think of something they hadn't considered.

Thankfully he did. "It's safe to assume Wish didn't plan on visiting the *Liberty Post* or injuring Snoops," he said. "She should've grabbed Birdie's Vette and headed straight for the lake to total it. Which begs the question—after Wish stole the car, why risk driving by the barn?"

Hector shrugged. "She wanted to see the newspaper. It's also where you and Birdie live." After a beat, he added, "Correction. It's where Birdie lives since you're living out of a suitcase."

Dodging the jab, Hugh stayed on point. "It was stupid and she's cunning. She knew auto theft would have the PD canvassing the area. She risked being caught in the commission of a crime."

"I think you're on to something," Hector said. He grew animated. "When I was in Iraq, HQ screwed up and stationed two brothers in the same troop. The gaffe was caught, and the younger brother was put on the first transport out. Rule number one of warfare. Never mix family."

"My point exactly," Hugh said. "Wish will try to stick to a plan. Her emotions for Birdie will get in the way. The daughter she raised to be a criminal just like Mama has settled down and gone straight. Maybe she sees it as an insult to the criminal code. Anything's possible."

The deduction appeared to please Hector. "What if we use Birdie as bait? Draw Wish out so she goes after her daughter? Might be an easy way to capture her."

The suggestion drove Birdie to her feet.

She flattened her palm on the wall as if the gravity beneath her feet had become unstable. Her violet eyes grew wide as she took in air she released with a sputtering sound.

Ignoring the men, she sent a look of entreaty to Theodora. "I'm as upset about this as anyone, but I'm not being used as bait. You don't know my mother. I've never crossed her, no one *ever* crosses her—and for good reason."

Ethel Lynn, worrying the nubby fabric of her jacket, rushed to Birdie's side. "Good heavens, don't fret," she said. "We won't let anything happen to you."

"If they use me as bait, how will you protect me?"

"The men were just batting around ideas. It was a ridiculous suggestion. No one will put you in harm's way." Ethel Lynn turned to Theodora. "Isn't that right? Tell her, Theodora."

The need to calm Birdie seemed less urgent because Hugh eased past Ethel Lynn and reached for his distraught fiancé. His attempt to comfort was thwarted as Birdie stepped back. After the way they'd been acting toward one another, her response was understandable. Her rejection bowed his shoulders and stole the light from his eyes. Somehow he pulled himself together, brushing off the hurt that surely cost him a great deal.

"Birdie, we were just thinking out loud," he said with false cheer. "It was a stupid idea we would've discarded after further consideration. Don't worry, all right? On my honor, I won't let Wish get within a mile of you."

"Count on it," Hector put in.

Birdie offered Hector a fleeting smile before throwing her attention on Hugh. "If that's your way of saying you're moving back in, forget it," she said. "I'm doing fine without you."

Hugh restrained the nasty rejoinder he seemed prepared to issue. "Sweetheart, I shouldn't have moved out," he said, his jaw working hard as he fought for patience—an attribute he didn't have in abundance. "I wouldn't have gone if I'd known your mother was tracking you. It never dawned on me that she'd try something as ballsy as driving by the *Liberty Post* to get a fix on where you live."

"Meaning it would've been okay to walk out on me if she *wasn't* a threat? Talk about cold comfort. You sure aren't reliable, are you?"

"You're twisting my words." He rolled his shoulders, no doubt to release the frustration building inside him when Birdie refused to meet his gaze. Softly, he added, "We'll work on our problems later. For now, it's best if I'm with you."

"No, it's not."

Clearly a lie, but the anger in her voice was more a

reflection of her fear than a salty rebuff of her beloved. It was time to intervene before either said anything they'd regret.

Slowly Theodora eased out of her chair. Lovers' quarrels made her weary right down to her bones, and left her wondering if most folks were incapable of enjoying happiness. Birdie and Hugh were the fortunate recipients of a match made in heaven—when they weren't busy warping their relationship into a deal struck in hell.

Youth was a dangerous business with its bounty of rash decisions and false pride. Were they unaware of how much they risked by neglecting to safeguard the love they shared? It was a priceless bounty, as rare as human kindness between strangers.

With the lightest touch, Theodora skimmed her fingers across Birdie's cheek. "Haven't I said you fret over the damnedest things?" she asked, trying to add honey to her voice. It was a hardship for a woman seasoned with too much vinegar. "You're in no more danger than I am. Everything is under control."

"You think so?" Hugging herself, Birdie began rocking like a child driven awake by nightmares. "My mother *will* figure out you're one of our long lost relatives—the relative who inherited the rubies. She probably already knows."

"It's no secret. So she knows. I don't give a damn."

"What makes you sure she won't come after us both?"

"Let her try." Theodora patted her buckskin satchel. "I'm armed and cranky at all times."

The stab at humor fell flat. "Maybe I should pack up and leave," Birdie said. "The town will be safer without me. So will you. If I go, my mother will follow. I'm sure of it."

"What nonsense. This is your home, child. You aren't going anywhere."

Hugh readily agreed. "Wish isn't making you give

up the first real home you've ever known," he said, with heat. "If we allow it, she gets the upper hand. And I won't stand for it, not ever. I swear I'll never let her hurt you again."

Theodora gave a *harrumph* of approval. Hugh might be temperamental but he adored Birdie. He simply wasn't confident about showing it. Not that Birdie made it easy. She had a nasty predisposition to suspect any binding expressions of love; understandable for a girl raised by con artists and thieves. Wish and the others who'd plagued Birdie's childhood knew nothing about loyalty or devotion. They certainly didn't have ethics. They'd raised Birdie to be one of them, but she was destined for something better. She always had been.

Returning to the task at hand, Theodora mapped out a strategy.

"Hector, you'll stay with Birdie. She has a nice guest bedroom. Stay close at all times. I don't want another mishap like what happened to Snoops." When Hugh started to object, she said to him, "Move your crap out of Anthony's house. Go back home to Birdie. I don't give a damn if you argue with her from dawn to dusk. Just help us find Wish. If she's crazy enough to run Snoops off the road, there's no telling what she'll do next."

"I don't want him back," Birdie interjected with childish petulance. Embarrassed by the outburst—which caused Snoops to stir in her slumber—she lowered her voice. "He wanted to move out? Fine by me. Let him stay where he is."

Irritation jangled across Theodora's skin. "I don't give a rat's ass what you want. The newspaper needs *both* its owners under one roof. Your new employees are still on a learning curve, and I won't see the *Post* go under because you're in the middle of a lovers' spat. Make him sleep on the floor it you like."

"With pleasure."

Theodora's cell phone hummed in her pocket. Excusing herself, she marched into the hospital corridor for privacy and a breath of air that wasn't fouled by quarreling lovers or male testosterone. If Wish planned to divide and conquer, she was well on her way.

Flipping open her cell, Theodora scanned the text. Incredulous, she muttered choice words. Tension shot straight through her bones.

The message read, *Earn your liberty . . . if you dare.*

Chapter 6

Hunched over the computer, Birdie called up tomorrow's edition of *The Liberty Post*.

It was past 10 P.M., and the final proof was late to the printer. She rechecked the lead about Mayor Ryan's battle to rezone the streets west of Liberty Square for commercial use. The article wouldn't make the front page in a metropolitan area, but the locals in this Ohio town protected residential areas with an admirable ferocity. Chopping down a mature tree was tantamount to murder. Council members went to lengths to ensure every road widened or new development built caused the least damage to the emerald necklace of forest surrounding Liberty.

Birdie's thoughts wended back to Snoops. The brainy preteen could've been killed in the accident. Why had Wish played vehicular chicken with a child? Poor Snoops—in the terrifying moments before her bicycle crashed to the ground, had she thought Birdie was behind the wheel? Had she believed an adult she trusted would cause her harm? The prospect filled Birdie with remorse and a nearly uncontrollable rage at her mother. How could Wish stoop so low she'd harm a child?

From across the newsroom, Hugh said, "You don't have to check the copy. It's done."

Yanked from her musings, she turned in the direction of his voice. He sauntered into the center of the barn, pausing before the rows of desks. Hector came in behind him.

She logged off the computer. "When did you have time to proof tomorrow's edition?" she asked, certain he'd forgotten the task. "We spent hours at the hospital."

"The last two stringers we interviewed? I hired them. They took care of it."

He'd hired more employees without consulting her? As partners, they'd agreed to make all major decisions together. The fact that he'd gone ahead without her approval seemed further evidence of their disintegrating relationship.

The regret she felt seemed a good companion for the rage at her mother, but she refused to let the volatile mix tap into the more vulnerable emotions jostling inside her. Better to stay angry, and prepared for whatever happened next. Knowing her mother, they wouldn't have long to wait.

She gazed at him challengingly. "Thanks for making unilateral management decisions. Are the new hires taking care of everything? Should I take the week off? Take up tennis or something? I'm not needed here, so what the hell."

The assault made Hugh flinch. "Sure, whatever you'd like," he said evenly. "Tomorrow go with Theodora to meet with the bounty hunter from North Carolina. Or spend the day with the women at The Second Chance. If you aren't up to working, it's understandable."

"You can't handle the newspaper without me—"

"I can," he said, cutting her off. "You've got enough on your plate. Let me worry about the newspaper and Wish. Birdie, I *will* protect you."

She stared at him, incredulous. "An hour ago you were planning to use me for bait. If that's your idea of protection, you're way off the mark."

Reaching the desk, Hector sat his suitcase on the floor before elbowing his way between them. "Play fair," he told her. "He didn't come up with the stupid idea. *I* suggested using you for bait."

Hugh laughed. "Are you *defending* me, pal? Shit, I didn't see that coming."

"I'm taking responsibility for a bad idea. I think they call it maturity."

"Good for you. I wasn't happy about taking the fall."

Hector spied the candy jar on Snoops' desk. "Let's try this," he said, strolling up. "How about a truce? The way I see it, if we take Birdie out of the equation we'll get along fine."

Hugh's mouth tightened. "I'm not following."

"Listen, I'm all for chasing a beautiful woman, but I don't chase if she's taken. I'm a stand-up guy." He dug a chocolate from the jar and tore off the wrapper.

A whisper of relief crossed Hugh's face. "Good to know."

"Does this mean we're friends?"

"No."

"Give me bonus points for trying." Popping the candy into his mouth, Hector zeroed in on Birdie. "Since we're on the subject of territorial habits, I have a question. If that asshole is on the outs with you, why are you still wearing his ring? Talk about mixed signals."

Coming up with a response would've been easy if not for the lump forming in her throat.

She was still wearing Hugh's ring because she belonged to him, body and soul. Wasn't she responsible for putting their relationship on shaky ground? Since they'd moved in together Hugh had tried to lock her down to a wedding date, using hints and direct questions when he'd tired of her evasions. She'd continually stalled, coming up with excuses on why they should wait.

What, exactly, was she waiting for—a sign he'd remain true for life? A money-back guarantee? On an intellectual level she understood the fragility of relationships, how a successful marriage took time and nurturing and probably more dedication than she could imagine.

But her doubts ran deeper.

She was frightened of investing herself completely, of trusting Hugh with every ounce of her love. If her devotion wasn't reciprocated, how to survive the disappointment? For someone who'd lived life on the fly, she wasn't much of a gambler.

To Hector she said, "I'm still wearing his ring because he hasn't asked for it back. Not yet anyway."

The comment sent Hugh's gaze to the floor. He studied his shoes like he'd never seen them before.

Hector nodded sagely. "So you'll keep his ring unless he wants it back?"

"Sure."

"Smart girl." He elbowed Hugh, drawing a glare. "You aren't dumb enough to break it off, are you? Think, man. She's one of kind. You'll never find another woman who comes close."

Hugh reached into the bottom drawer of his desk. "Aren't you the guy who's twice divorced?" He found a bottle of Jack Daniels and a glass. Downing a shot, he added, "Improve your batting average before you give me tips."

"Low blow, pal. I didn't ask for divorce. *They* did."

"Both times? Hell, you are a loser."

"I'm unlucky in love. It happens."

Birdie snatched the glass and poured a shot for Hector. "Why did your wives divorce you?" she asked, handing it over. He'd gone blue around the edges, piquing her interest.

"Long story. Not worth telling."

"C'mon, you're among friends. Well, one friend and a grouch."

Hugh scratched his armpit. "I am not a grouch."

Hector poured acid into his smile. "You sound like Nixon when you say that." He studied the glass, swirling the amber liquid. From over the rim, he told Birdie, "If you want the God's honest truth, I have a thing for damsels in distress."

Fairytales weren't prominent in her background, and she wasn't sure she understood. "Like you want to rescue women?" she asked. "Princesses who've taken a liking to poison apples and stuff like that?" It was nice, actually.

"More or less." He downed the shot then scowled at Hugh. "I'd rather not go into the details. Romeo will hit me with an insult and I won't like it. Don't let the calm exterior fool you. I'm an emotional guy."

Hugh smirked. "You mean you're a cream puff."

"Watch it."

The phone rang.

Hugh beat her to it, snatching up the receiver. She heard shouting, a real fireworks display. Women in labor didn't make as much noise as the guy on the other end. His mouth thinning, Hugh murmured soothing words that appeared to go unheard.

Hanging up, he said, "That was the bounty hunter from North Carolina. He's not coming."

The niggling sensation Birdie had come to detest started up her spine. "Why not? Theodora is expecting him."

"He quit."

"He can't!"

"He just talked to his wife. Their house was ransacked while she was at work. Think Mongols galloping across the Asian Steppe and a house in ruins. Wish left a note promising more trouble if he didn't quit the case. The note was written in red nail polish. A nice touch."

Hector grabbed the whiskey, poured. "Wait a second. Wish is here in Liberty. How did she break into a house in North Carolina?"

Birdie took the shot before it reached his lips and chugged. After the fire cleared her throat, she said. "My mother has friends, the seediest people imaginable. She got the name of the bounty hunter and paid someone to ransack his home. The perfect scare tactic."

An even more worrisome thought intruded. It was the kind of thought sure to make an awful day end on a dreadful note.

She slid the phone toward Hugh. "You have the phone numbers for the other bounty hunters, right?" she asked. "Call them. Make sure no one else drops out."

He stared at her, incredulous. "Your mother can't scare them all off the case. How can she get the name of every man hired?"

"And woman," Hector put in. "I saw the photos attached to Theodora's list. She brought in a woman from Milwaukee who could box as a heavyweight. I wouldn't last three rounds with her. You wouldn't either, Hugh."

"Whatever. All I'm saying is Wish doesn't have the means to find every bounty hunter on her tail. She's not a freaking magician."

"Not on her own, she doesn't," Birdie said. "But the FBI can find virtually anyone. They can track down everyone Theodora hired."

The disclosure sent an uneasy tension whipping through the office.

Why broach an embarrassing subject? Most of Birdie's childhood memories resided uneasily at the bottom of her heart, rarely visited and never enjoyed. Some of the memories were a sheer torment. Yet the men needed every bit of her terrible knowledge.

Hugh leaned against the desk with the wary movements of a man preparing for bad news. Hector, too, remained silent, his eyes hooded.

She marshaled her thoughts then said, "When my mother isn't working a more elaborate con she preys on men. Usually she picks a man grieving the death of his wife or someone who's just lonely."

Hugh grunted. "Old news. She targets a wealthy man in a small town and pretends she'll marry the dupe. Then she cleans out his savings, robs his jewelry store or steals a ride from his car dealership—whatever she can get her hands on."

"Like she did with Birdie's father, the guy she didn't know *was* her father." Hector's lips moved silently as he fished around in his brain. "Landon Williams, right? He still lives here, although I hope no one's told him about our present situation."

"He doesn't know about Wish," Hugh said grimly. "Landon struggles with depression. Learning that the woman who ruined him has returned . . . it isn't something he needs to know."

Birdie put in, "I talked to Meade. She had relatives in Chicago invite Landon for a stay. He left this morning."

"Who's Meade?" Hector asked.

"Landon's daughter," Hugh explained. "Meade is Birdie's half-sister."

"Single?"

"You have a one-track mind." To Birdie, Hugh said, "What are you driving at? We know your mother uses men."

"You know she uses vulnerable men. There's more to it. A lot more."

A sensation like suffocation bore down on her. The memories followed, a tumult of images rising as quickly as her fear. She recalled the man in the dark sedan who'd

85

smelled of cigarettes and well-coiled rage. Then a second memory accosted her, of a tight-lipped giant with a forehead so massive it had reminded a five-year-old Birdie of a dinosaur egg in a favorite storybook. The giant had carried a sidearm longer than her arm.

In the dim recesses of her mind, she recalled how he'd barked an order for her to sit still. She'd been fidgeting on a bench in a park that could've been in Tampa or Phoenix or San Diego—the specifics were no longer clear. What *did* stick through the years was the brutal way he shoved her mother down the sidewalk, the stiletto heels on her pumps screeching as she thrashed desperately in his hold. The sight of Wish as a helpless victim—her mother, who brought men to their knees and crafted horrible punishments for her daughter's slightest infractions—had filled Birdie with an emptiness so deep, she might have drowned in it.

Throughout childhood she'd understood there were two types of men. The harmless sort called her 'sweet baby' and treated her like a princess. The others were as affectionate as a shark.

Bringing her attention back to Hugh and Hector, she said, "My mother doesn't only con decent men. She keeps lovers in law enforcement, the type who have no interest in upholding the law. The worst sort. I think one of the men works at the FBI, probably in Washington. She's always been keen on visiting DC a few times a year. That's why she's never caught. Her lover—or lovers, there might be more than one at the federal level—they give her a head's up whenever she's at risk of being apprehended."

The explanation rolled over Hugh like a tsunami. "Your mother keeps lovers *in the FBI?*"

"Police, too. I saw a lot of badges growing up but never got any names. Maybe she's not sleeping with an Ohio State Trooper, but an officer from New York or California? She's good at strategy."

Blinking, Hector took it all in. "So she *does* have a way to get the name of every bounty hunter. This is not good. We need to warn Theodora."

"She won't care. She's convinced we'll catch Wish."

"That's optimistic," Hector said. "For all we know, Wish has the Feds tapping Theodora's cell. If she's heating up the sheets with a G-man, why not? It would be at the top of her to-do list."

"And tapping our phones." Hugh examined his cell like it carried typhus. "It won't do any good to get replacements, not if she has someone in the FBI listening in. From here on out, no important conversations unless we're standing in front of each other—preferably outside."

"Works for me," Hector agreed.

Hugh sent a black look. "Gee, pal. You're taking this in stride. Wish probably has you targeted like the rest of us."

"She won't come near me. I'm untouchable."

"Says who?"

"Uncle Nick, that's who."

"Who's he?"

"The big brother of my late mother, bless her soul." Digging back into the candy jar, Hector selected a red jellybean. He tossed it from hand to hand. "Outside of family reunions and weddings, I steer clear of Uncle Nick. He runs a trucking company and a few other businesses no one in my family talks about. All I know is he keeps us protected. Once my cousin Dimitri rammed his Toyota into a Philly lawyer's Mercedes. Big lawsuit threatened— Dimitri was shitting bricks. Then Spider paid the good counselor a visit. The lawsuit disappeared."

"Spider?"

"Uncle Nick's assistant. Scary guy, bigger than this barn. I kid you not—he's got a tattoo of a black widow spider right on his kisser. Creepy looking thing. If my Uncle Nick has directed him to send a few Philly deadheads to sleep with the fishes, I wouldn't be surprised."

Hugh stepped back, knocking into the desk. "Sleep with the fishes . . . what is this, *The Godfather?* You're saying your uncle is a member of the Italian mafia?"

"Italians, Greeks—we mingle. But basically, yes." Hector winked at Birdie. "Babe, I don't care if Wish and her friends chase the other bounty hunters into the hills. I'm on the case."

"I'm not your babe," she said, moving the candy dish out of his reach. He was naturally high-strung without the sugar. "Still, I appreciate the sentiment. And your Uncle Nick's protection, if that's what you call it. I'm glad you're staying on the case."

"I'd ask him to send goons to nab your mother, but I it wouldn't end well."

The thought of her mother behind bars made Birdie heartsick, but at least Wish deserved incarceration. "I'm frightened of my mother, especially her vindictive streak, but I don't want her harmed. Do you mind if we leave Uncle Nick out of this?"

Hector gave the thumbs up. "Glad we're on the same wavelength."

The doorbell *chime, chime, chimed* through the house.

Startled by the sound, Theodora spattered droplets of chamomile tea across her robe. On the nightstand, the clock read 11:35 P.M.

Setting down the teacup, she hoisted herself from the rocking chair in her bedroom and tromped through the house flicking on lights and muttering choice words that merely increased the pace of her rickety heart.

She hadn't been herself since receiving the alarming text message at the hospital, a cryptic threat from the damnable Wish. It had seemed wise to keep the message a secret, at least until she ruminated on the meaning.

Earn your liberty . . . if you dare.

Did Wish intend to run her off the road as she'd done to defenseless Snoops? Theodora wasn't well acquainted with fear, at least not the fear of bodily harm. But for the first time in memory she considered loading her Saturday Night Special *and* her Winchester rifle with real ammo.

Spitting choice words, she threw open the door.

Without awaiting an invitation, Ethel Lynn sashayed past. "Does your hearing aid need a tune-up?" she inquired. "I thought you'd never answer."

She shrugged out of her trench coat, a strange affair of purple satin with hot pink piping. But it was her choice of clothing underneath that gave Theodora pause. She wore a silky nightgown and matching robe of electric blue.

"Ethel Lynn, go home. I'm not having a slumber party." Spending the night with her lifelong nemesis made a quick death by coronary sound good.

"Stop your griping. I'm here and that's that."

She slid off her boots and placed them neatly against the wall. With a flourish she withdrew bunny slippers from the satchel she carried. The slippers, with droopy pink ears and black button eyes, seemed better suited for an adolescent. Which, come to think of it, described Ethel Lynn most days.

"Are the sheets clean in the spare bedroom?" she asked. "I refuse to sleep in a pigsty."

"How the hell would I know? I wasn't expecting company. Now, leave."

"Oh, put a sock in it." Ethel Lynn steered her feet into the slippers and clicked her heels like a girl in the Emerald City. "All better. Do you have Earl Grey?"

"I'm all out."

"Chamomile? Something soothing?"

89

"For you? Hell, no."

"It's for the best. I need something stronger. It's been an upsetting day, what with Snoops being injured and your inability to catch Wish. Really, Theodora—what's the point of hiring bounty hunters if they don't hunt?"

Fury sizzled across the synapses in Theodora's brain. She scanned the foyer for the broom. It was time to shoo Ethel Lynn out.

The doorbell rang.

Finney Smith, The Second Chance Grill's hot-tempered cook, shoved her way inside, filling the house with bustling impatience. In her early forties, with a lousy blonde coloring job on her thick hair, she was as curvaceous as any woman alive. She was also gruff, tough and usually more irritable than Theodora, a feat unto itself.

Evidently the cook was also spending the night—beneath her frayed navy jacket, she wore striped pajamas that must've belonged to her late husband.

She whipped her finger through the air. "Don't even start," she said, halting the digit beneath Theodora's nose. "You're not staying alone after what happened to Snoops. I'd ask if you've mentioned the danger to your kids or grandkids, any of whom would protect you, but I know your stubborn streak makes you stupid."

Theodora shimmied her shoulders in a burst of irritation. "Hello to you too, Finney." The cook wasn't tall but Theodora was even shorter. This left her glaring at a generous pair of breasts. "I'm not running a halfway house for single women. Go home to your children."

"My children are nearly adults. They're fine."

"I mean it. Go, and take *that* with you." She nodded in Ethel Lynn's general direction.

Finney hung her coat in the foyer closet. "Why didn't I pack a frying pan? You need some sense knocked into you."

"Will you take cash? I'll pay you to leave."

90

"Not unless the cash is taped to a man six feet tall. I could use one of those."

"Keep dreaming. I'm as liable to start a dating service as send love letters to Ethel Lynn."

Ethel Lynn rearranged the feathery wisps of her hair. "A card at Christmas would be nice," she said to Theodora. "You're the only person I know who doesn't spread holiday cheer. It doesn't make the top ten, but I think it's a sin."

"When do I ever spread cheer?" Giving up, she marched to the living room and the salvation of liquor.

Finney beat her to the bar. "Have you talked to Mayor Ryan?" The cook studied the bottles arranged on the glass shelf, eventually selecting an aged Scotch.

"Not since yesterday. Why?"

Ethel Lynn's bunny slippers twitched. "Heavens, I forgot about the mayor. I haven't seen her that upset since the county commissioner dumped her for Judge Gilmore's secretary."

"Genevieve something-or-other," Finney said of the secretary. She studied her size ten shoes. "I hate tiny women. They get all the men with their batty eyelashes and petite bodies." The cook studied Theodora. "You don't count. You're only small on the outside. What you lack in size you make up for in sheer rage."

The conversation was at risk of devolving into a discussion about men and the tiny women they loved, a favorite topic of the well-fleshed Finney. What she needed was a lumberjack, a man with a hearty appetite for pancakes *and* earthly delights. Sadly enough, Theodora hadn't seen any in Ohio since the Johnson Administration.

Steering back on course, she prodded, "What's got Mayor Ryan in a huff?"

"The calls coming in to the courthouse," Finney supplied. "One after another. The mayor has received more complaints than her staff can handle."

Ethel Lynn took her drink and flitted over to the couch. "Mayor Ryan must've received a dozen calls this afternoon."

"Who's complaining to the mayor?" Theodora asked. After staying with Snoops at the hospital, she'd gone straight home.

Neither of the intruders was eager to explain. The glance they traded left Theodora with the impression there'd been trouble in town. What had Wish done now?

Finney settled in an easy chair beside the fireplace's last glowing embers. "Some of the complaints are about a pickpocket," she said. "Or pickpockets."

"There's more than one?" Worried, Theodora wondered if they'd been mistaken in thinking the mistress of disguise worked solo. Had Wish brought a crew with her?

The cook rested her head against the chair's soft cushion and closed her eyes. "Everyone says Wish is tricky with her disguises, but I can't believe she's capable of impersonating a youth barely out of high school. The police received two of the complaints within minutes, one from a pedestrian in the center green and another from a secretary in one of the law offices on The Square. Cash lifted from both parties, but the descriptions of the thieves don't match. One pickpocket was the young man I mentioned. The other was a woman."

"That *does* sound like more than one thief. Even if Wish is working in disguise she can't change her costume within minutes." At least Theodora hoped she couldn't.

"It gets worse," Finney said. "The mayor received a call from the owner of the craft store. Late this afternoon the cash register was cleaned out—more than five hundred dollars stolen. No one's sure how it happened with three employees working and customers milling in the aisles. The police asked the shop owners on The Square to remain vigilant."

"It's not enough. They need to get the word out to every business in Liberty. Wish probably targeted The Square to draw the police. They'll waste precious manpower guarding the shops while she spreads out across town." Theodora sipped her Scotch. To no one in particular, she added, "The devil sent me a text message."

Ethel Lynn gasped.

She began fanning herself with a magazine snatched from the coffee table, a dog-eared copy of *Field and Stream*. Finney, who seemed made of the cast iron she preferred in her skillets, opened her eyes and lowered her brows. "What did Wish say?" she asked.

"I'm not sure what she meant."

"Don't keep us on tenterhooks! What was the message?"

Theodora released a soft, ragged expulsion of air. "Earn your liberty if you dare. Lord and Jezebel—how am I supposed to know what it means?"

In the fireplace a log popped, startling them all. A thin thread of flame circled the log before dying back down.

Finney, emptying her glass, went to the bar for a refill. After she poured, she stood with her palms flat on the bar's marble surface.

There was something comforting in her stance, in the way she squared her shoulders and lifted her chin as if preparing for combat. She was decades younger than Ethel Lynn or Theodora, a tough woman who'd known her share of hard knocks, including the death of the police officer she'd married and a youthful widowhood struggling to raise her son and daughter on a cook's wages.

She wore gently used clothes bought at thrift shops, and her hands were covered with nicks from hard work. Yet Finney never complained about the life she'd been meted out by an unlucky fate or the exhaustion she felt while shepherding two sassy teenagers toward adulthood. It occurred to Theodora that she was glad the cook had come to spend the night, even if it meant the dizzy Ethel Lynn had arrived as well.

Returning to her chair, Finney said, "The message isn't about you, Theodora. It's a threat about taking what you most cherish."

"I cherish lots of things. What are you driving at?"

"Wish knows you love the town. She probably knows how much of your wealth goes to the school, churches and local groups. Just last month you gave a thousand dollars to the food bank run by First Baptist. You're Liberty's greatest benefactor. Always have been."

Most of those donations were made privately, and it was surprising Finney had come by the specific information regarding First Baptist. No doubt she'd overheard customers flapping their gums at The Second Chance Grill. In Theodora's estimation, she was simply giving back to the town that had provided for her family clear back to her ancestor Justice Postell, the freed slave who'd arrived from South Carolina during the Civil War. The Hendricks clan owed much to Liberty.

Withdrawing from her thoughts, she gave Finney a long look. "So Wish knows I take care of my town. What's your point?"

"She means to make you earn Liberty back."

"Finney, I don't *own* the town. How can I earn back something if it isn't mine?"

"By making Wish leave. She leaves, and there are no more complaints about pickpockets or shops losing cash from the till. Kids like Snoops will be safe. Life will go on as usual."

"And Birdie won't be scared anymore," Theodora murmured. The girl was frightened to the bone. If Wish left, she'd finish building a decent future from the ash of her former life. She deserved the chance.

Ethel Lynn, quiet until now, said, "I imagine Wish hates you for helping her daughter. Birdie was heading down the wrong track until you turned her life around." The dim bulb in her brain suddenly brightened. "Lordy, I just had a thought. Since you're Birdie's long-lost kin, you're also related to Wish." She shivered. "I think I'd rather be dead."

Ants seemed to wriggle beneath Theodora's skin. She squirmed in her chair. "Ethel Lynn, if I haven't said it enough, let me be clear. I hate you. It's just like you to remind me of something nasty."

"I merely state fact. Wish *is* part of your family tree."

"Prune her off," Finney said, "with a chain saw."

Anger climbed Theodora's back. Damn if she'd spend thirty seconds ruminating about the bloodline she shared with an alley cat. "Ethel Lynn, why don't you sit quietly and get drunk? It's none of your beeswax if I've suffered the misfortune of a family tie with Wish Kaminsky."

"That's not all you'll suffer," Ethel Lynn said, lifting her drink with a celebratory wave. "Wish plans to blackmail you something awful. She must be furious. You've made Birdie rich by sharing the rubies. Hasn't Wish been searching for her family treasure for years? Isn't that why Birdie came to Liberty in the first place?"

"The gems belong to my family too. I wouldn't share them with a thief even if you stuck needles in my eyes."

"I don't know about sharing, but I'm happy to cause you injury. Where's your embroidery case?"

"Oh, shut up."

Deaf to their bickering, Finney asked, "What if Ethel Lynn's right? I hate to agree with her on anything, but she has a point. What if Wish makes you buy back Liberty's freedom? Will you pay if it means she'll go?"

The question roused the meager fury Ethel Lynn hid in her belly. "Have you lost your mind?" she cried, gathering her hands to her withered breasts. "Let Wish get away with blackmail and where will it end? In a year or two she'll come back to cause trouble all over again unless Theodora gives her more cash. We won't do it!"

Theodora nodded in assent. "Damn right. Wouldn't do to give in. The hunger poisoning Wish can't be sated. Why even try?"

Finney's brows almost cleared her hairline. "Color me surprised. Never thought I'd live long enough to see you two agree on anything."

Chapter 7

Hugh fetched a spare blanket from the hallway closet and beat a resigned path to the living room. The lights were off, probably taken care of by Hector on his way to the guest bedroom. Moonlight filled the room with an eerie glow.

In the master suite Birdie was finishing off her bedtime routine, running water and banging through drawers with enough focus to drive anyone off. She expected him to sleep on the couch, a fit punishment for moving out of the apartment last week.

Defiance nudged him back into the hallway.

To do her bidding seemed an act of cowardice, an indication he couldn't face the end result of a poor decision. Their relationship, tenuous at the best of times, was now damaged further by a course of action that, in retrospect, he'd made without careful consideration. Hurting the woman he loved was never his aim.

As shadows collected around his legs in swaths of grey, he wondered if he'd reacted like a child, thinking the abandonment would shock Birdie into agreeing to set a date for their wedding. Now, the clumsy ultimatum filled him with shame.

How to patch things up? Returning to the bedroom

was a good place to start.

Grabbing a pillow from the bed, he tossed it on the floor and spread out the spare blanket. The room was even messier than before he'd moved out. Magazines and fast food boxes were heaped at the foot of the bed. Sweet-smelling laundry sat in a rumpled heap inside a laundry basket, but he resisted the urge to fold it. He'd just crawled beneath the blanket when Birdie came out of the bathroom in a flannel nightgown as enticing as a root canal.

She snapped back the comforter. "You're sleeping on the floor? I haven't vacuumed."

She hadn't dusted either, but he wasn't going there. "I'm fine. All tucked in."

"Hugh, the floor's a mess. By morning you'll be covered in dust bunnies and ants."

It seemed like a free pass that she hadn't mentioned the couch. "I don't mind," he assured her. No guts, no glory, and so he asked, "Is it all right if I stay? If you want me to go . . ."

"I don't care what you do."

She doused the light, surrounding them in blackness.

Hugh lowered his head to the pillow and stared, unseeing, at the ceiling. Acute discomfort had a way of heightening the senses, and he listened for the slowing of her breathing, an indication she'd drifted off. Instead, a prickly tension gathered in the air. His eyes adjusting, he caught sight of the comforter sliding left then right. The sheet, which appeared the color of charcoal in the diminished light, rippled above him as she mumbled unintelligible words.

More thrashing, and he took the opening.

"Do you remember during the holidays, when we started planning the newspaper?" he asked, rushing toward the safe ground of shared memory. "Tromping through the snow to look at properties? Total whiteout conditions. We were so pumped about finding the perfect building, we didn't mind the weather. The realtor thought we were nuts."

"Maybe we were," Birdie offered with faint peevishness.

Undeterred, he kept his voice light. "Who cares about buying real estate between Christmas and New Year's, right? I felt sorry for the realtor when we insisted on driving out to the barn on New Year's Eve. We'd already looked at ten places. It was snowing so hard, and we made her late for a party."

Hugh smiled into the dark. The barn they'd renovated had been on the market for two years, a neglected property annexed from one of the larger farms in the county after the owner fell on hard times. They'd waded through snowdrifts to get inside, the realtor trying to look cheery as she ruined her leather pumps on the trek. Hugh and Birdie had dressed more sensibly in heavy parkas and boots.

"The realtor thought we were wasting her time," he added, recalling his first glimpse inside the huge structure, the cobwebs hanging across stalls that once housed a dozen horses and the faint scent of leather in the tack room. He'd fallen in love on sight. "I knew we'd found the right place, somewhere big enough to grow a county newspaper." He declined to add he'd also known it was the perfect place to build a foundation for his new life with her.

"Remember how you started marking off where we'd put the offices?" she asked.

"I knew exactly how we'd lay it all out."

More rustling from above, and she moved closer to the edge of the bed. "You were sketching out the layout on the drive back into town."

Her nearness emboldened him. "Birdie, I shouldn't have rushed you," he said, an apology rimming the words. "Getting engaged, opening the newspaper—it was too much, too fast. Too many responsibilities."

"You were a man on fire."

"You should've thrown a bucket of ice water on my head," he said ruefully. Her soft laughter wove through the air, earthy and warm, lending him the courage to add, "I didn't understand my good fortune when you said you'd marry me. Not the way I should have, not fully. Why didn't I treat you better? Why was I so blind to everything I had to gain? After we got engaged, I should've taken you away for a few weeks. On a cruise or to a sandy beach. We needed time to cement our relationship."

"You were in a hurry."

"I was born in a hurry." He wasn't sure why. Then he jumped at the logical explanation. "I've seen too many people waste time, me included. Waste chances. Life goes by fast. Delay too long and you miss the best opportunities."

"You're afraid of middle age."

The observation rang uncomfortably true. "You think so?" he asked, valuing her opinion.

"Hugh, you're almost forty. It's normal."

"I wasted too much time when I was younger. Now I'm afraid of missing the rest. Still, it doesn't give me reason for being hard on you."

"You have to stop judging me," she said, and the emotion in her voice heightened his sense of shame. "Less than a year ago I was roaming from state to state. Now everything is different. I've inherited more cash than I know what to do with, and I own half of a newspaper. Maybe I even have a future with my business partner, a shot at something real, but I'm still learning how to do this."

"You *do* have a future with your business partner." His heart seized. She was everything to him, his lodestar. "If you want it."

"You don't make it easy. You're like a drill

sergeant," she said, choking back sobs. Her despair cut him deep. Pulling herself together, she added, "In some ways you're like my mother. You took off when times got tough. You left without stopping to think how much it would hurt me. I'm not blaming you. I know I'm not easy to live with. But you shouldn't cut and run at the first sign of trouble. Couples have problems—it comes with the territory. They should try to work it out. You didn't."

Harsh words and he deserved every one.

He *had* cut and run. He'd moved out without knowing Wish would upend Birdie's ordered life. He'd abandoned his betrothed when she needed him most.

"I swear I'll never make that mistake again. Birdie, I promise." He reached toward the bed in hopes of clasping her fingers and putting form to the vow. Nothing but empty space greeted him, a void where he'd snuffed out her trust through one careless act. Drawing on the belief he'd find a way to heal their relationship, he added, "I'm not usually impulsive. Then again, I've never loved a woman the way I love you. Virgin territory, and I'm still learning how to negotiate my feelings. I'll do better."

"Try speaking up when I'm driving you crazy." A pause, then, "I'll stop throwing my stuff everywhere. Bad habit from my years living on the fly."

"I'd appreciate it." Needing to indulge her, he added, "If it's too much for you, we'll get someone in to help. Or I'll try to ignore the stuff on the floor."

"At least try to ignore some of it," she said. "I don't need anything else at the moment." She was alluding to Wish.

"Your mother won't stay in Liberty," he assured her. "Even her friends in law enforcement can't keep her one hundred percent safe. She'll move on."

"You think so?" A childlike hope surrounded the question.

"You know your mother. She blows through a town,

cons a few dupes and heads out. She won't deviate from her predictable course."

He prayed the words, meant to comfort, weren't the stuff of lies.

Somewhere inside the house, the two teenagers quarreled. The noise brought Wish to a halt in the driveway. From the sounds of it, the boy was winning the argument with his sister.

The house, a neglected dwelling located five miles outside Liberty, hid behind maple trees as if in embarrassment. Paint peeled in curls from the exterior, revealing pine planks underneath. Moss bled across the planks in vibrant green swirls as if the forest were intent on reclaiming the house from its hotheaded residents. The lawn wasn't much to look at with its patches of yellowing grass on the unforgiving earth. The mailbox looked like someone had taken a wrecking ball to it.

The domicile of a wage slave, Wish thought contemptuously. What did the owner get for her trouble? A rundown house she shared with her perpetually warring offspring.

Yesterday Wish had instructed her accomplices to watch the family. Throughout the day Beavis and Butthead took to the task with relish, snapping photos and stalking the trio. They'd learned the family's schedule, lending Wish a bead on the best time to strike.

Which was now. Ten minutes before the unsociable boy left for his job at the hardware store on The Square, and the girl, with her penchant for heavy eye shadow and cheap bangles, left for cheerleading practice at the high school.

Like most teenagers they would prove too self-absorbed to notice the truck parked on the road didn't bear the logo of a telecommunications corporation and the service woman, dressed smartly in a navy blue uniform, didn't have an appointment.

Stay focused.

Wish knew she didn't need another mishap like the one she'd experienced with Snoops. Driving too close to the kid's bicycle had been reckless, impulsive—out of character for a professional who understood the danger of a murder rap. If she'd gone too far none of her lovers could've shielded her from hard time, not even the G-man in the FBI's Washington bureau.

A surge of malice accompanied her up the steps.

It would've been simpler to break in while the house was empty, although not nearly as fun—or as devastating.

The best scams created a series of little deaths in other people's lives, a ripple of agony sure to linger after the crime. The robbery, by itself, wouldn't evoke adequate sorrow. But this particular target would learn she'd not only been visited by misfortune; her incautious children had ushered it inside.

More shouting, and Wish pulled open the screen door. "Hello? Anyone here?"

The boy plodded into the foyer. "What do you want?"

He was blessed with a man's loose-limbed sexuality. Regrettably it was paired with a youth's sullen demeanor. Dark hair fell around his face, shielding eyes that strayed to the tight curve of her shirt.

Wish offered a seductive smile. "Technician," she rapped out. "I'm here to install the Wi-Fi."

His disbelief at the news gave way to glee. "We're getting Wi-Fi?" he asked.

She snapped open the toolbox. In one of those nice coincidences she relished, she'd lifted it from the hardware store where he worked. "You'll have the fastest Internet service in Ohio, everything you need." She produced the fake order.

Predictably the boy didn't bother to read it. He called to his sister.

When she appeared in her pink cheerleading outfit, he asked, "Did Mom tell you we're getting Internet?" By the time he'd finished explaining, her round face was bright with irritation.

"Randy, I don't have time for this. We have to *go*." The girl gave Wish the once over. "Are you sure you have the right house? There's no way Mom would pay for Internet service."

"She's cheap," the boy said. "Totally embarrassing. I have to log on to my accounts from the school library."

"You won't have to now. This is a new package we're offering to select customers." Wish stole a glance at the living room. No cable box, and she relaxed as she spotted the landline phone on a table. The contraption looked older than the kids, with a black cord running toward the wall. "We want to help our customers upgrade, especially those in rural areas. There's no charge for the first six months."

The girl did a double take. "We're getting free service for six months?"

"Looks like your mother is having it installed as a surprise. Is it your birthday?"

"Not even close."

"Then it's because of the promotion. I've been working overtime since it started."

The explanation didn't quite wash with the girl. "Let me call her to make sure. She's at work."

A game of guts poker, and the danger spiked Wish's blood like a drug.

"Of course. Call your mother." She rubbed her wrist, feigning distress. "I really have to remember to wear my watch. I had trouble waking the kids this morning, we were all running late—do you have the time? This is my last stop today. I'm hoping to knock off by five. Or, if you prefer, I'll come back at another time. I'm sure I have an opening on my calendar for next month."

The boy took the bait. "Marla, forget about calling mom. It's almost four o'clock and if I'm late for work, my boss will kill me. Let's go."

"We can't leave a stranger in the house!"

Wish ran her tongue across her lips, drawing the boy's interest. "She doesn't look strange to me," he said, his ears turning as red as cherries. He dragged his sister close. "You're being a pill. Don't you want Internet service twenty-four seven? Any time you need it?" Hope gleamed in his eyes as he turned back to Wish. "Will it be working by the time we get home?"

"I'll have it up and running within the hour. And don't worry. I'll lock the door on my way out."

Theodora Hendricks pulled into the *Liberty Post's* parking lot in a 1960s Cadillac so sweet, Hector began to salivate. The ride was sky blue with polished tailfins and a vertically ribbed rear beauty panel. It looked as worthy of museum consideration as its owner.

She stuck her head out the driver side window. "Snap to," she barked. "I don't have all day."

Hector wondered if they'd scheduled an appointment he'd forgotten. Doubtful, which meant the old woman was following her own agenda. From harsh experience he knew to be wary of any woman with an agenda.

The day was definitely *not* starting out well. He'd just navigated his way through the newsroom, where Hugh was shouting orders at the journalists in his employ and Birdie, sullen from the moment she'd risen, was collecting her purse to go out. She'd refused to reveal where.

The lovebirds weren't getting along well, and

Hector knew their fragile relationship didn't need the extra stress Wish provided. Escaping the busy newsroom and working solo today had seemed an excellent idea.

With trepidation, he approached the Cadillac. "Your car's a beaut," he said to Theodora. "If Liberty hosts a summer parade, I'd make it the lead car."

"Liberty does, and it is. I never play second fiddle, not even in a parade."

Not much surprise there. She'd stand up to Napoleon if he were alive. Probably steal his funky hat and his troops too.

Switching topics, he asked, "Are you looking for Birdie? I can get her if you'd like."

"I'm not here to socialize with my kin." She unlocked the Cadillac's passenger door. "Get in."

With reservation he complied. "Are we going to breakfast?" He'd been dreaming of a three-egg omelet since daybreak. "I'll catch you up on my progress. There isn't much, but I'm glad to fill you in."

The banter wrinkled her brow. "Do I look like your mother?" she demanded with crotchety impatience. "If you don't have the sense to start the day proper, I'm not feeding you."

"Then what's up?"

"There's been a development. It's bad."

"Everything surrounding Wish Kaminsky is bad. What happened?"

"Three more bounty hunters quit. They've all suffered one misfortune or another, and received threats to boot."

"What were the threats?" He wondered if he should be writing this down.

"Oh, the usual love letters from the scoundrels Wish hired. Threats about destroying the bounty hunter's finances or preying on his relatives. The brother of one of the hunters is a Congressman from Alabama. Seems Wish had someone hack into his Twitter account."

"That's not so bad, is it?" Even so, Hector was grateful for his Uncle Nick's protection. If Wish dug around for scuttlebutt on the Levendakis tribe, she'd find the connection and back off. Having a mob boss for an uncle was an embarrassment, but it did have its perks. "There are worse tragedies for a Congressman than having his Twitter hacked. Given Wish's capabilities, he got off easy."

"You think? The Congressman is up for reelection. Wish had someone tweet quotes from *The Communist Manifesto*. I've known a few Alabama boys in my day, and they aren't fans of Marx."

"I wouldn't imagine."

"Now I've lost three more hunters. It just burns my biscuits." To emphasize her frustration she twitched her skinny hips like someone zapped by stray electricity.

"So we're going into battle with fewer troops," he said, wondering why the news about less competition didn't make him happy. He needed to reimburse his patient ex-wives and seething ex-fiancé the money he'd lost in the stock market—fewer hunters vying for the reward money should've thrilled him. It didn't, mostly because he was over his head with the bounty hunter job. How would a novice hunt her down?

Wish was a pro. She knew how to avoid capture. She slept with powerful men and never stayed anywhere long. Odds were, she'd evade the police and continue robbing Liberty's residents until she was ready to ride off into the sunset. She'd hurt law-abiding citizens and there wasn't a damn thing he could do about it.

The prospect of failing angered him. He liked the people Wish threatened and their quaint Ohio town. Theodora was a little hard on the nerves but he admired her take-no-prisoners attitude, a rare quality in a woman her age.

He also liked Snoops, the kid who'd broken her leg,

107

and Hugh, despite his less-than-welcoming behavior.

Most of all, he enjoyed Birdie's company. He couldn't imagine how she dealt with the knowledge her mother was heartless and cruel. A woman like Wish didn't deserve the distinction or the rewards that came with motherhood. She sure didn't deserve a daughter as nice as Birdie.

Getting back on track, he said, "Wish plans to scare off your entire crew. According to Birdie, she has friends in law enforcement *and* criminal networks. That's a lot of protection. If it's open season on Liberty, what's to stop her?"

"I don't know. What do you think we should do?"

"We? This is your party, Theodora. I only work here."

Merriment eased the lines in her face. "Yes, you do. As of today, I'm paying you to stay on the case. You will, won't you?"

The offer of a paycheck was welcome news. "Wish won't scare me off if that's what you're asking," he assured her. "I'm here for the duration."

"I figured you wouldn't quit." She gave an appraising look. "At the hospital with Snoops? You did a good job hiding how you felt, but I knew you were upset. Nice of you to have real human feeling for a child you hardly know. It tears me up to think she might have been killed. What was Wish thinking, driving like a maniac?"

"She *wasn't* thinking. Trying to run Snoops off the road was an impulse. She couldn't have known the kid would show up in the newspaper's parking lot. It was bad luck they arrived at the same time." He raked his hand across his scalp. "I hate reckless drivers."

"Lordy, I do too. Last summer a carload of local boys rammed a garbage truck on The Square right after midnight. Three sheets to the wind, all of them."

"Hurt?"

"A few broken bones. Chief Burnes was coming off his shift at the police department and happened to drive by. Fortunately for the boys, he called it in. They were out like lights."

"I'm glad they weren't seriously injured."

Dropping the subject, he willed away the memory of another accident before it swamped him.

He had a job to do this morning, and no time to grieve the past. Some mistakes were unforgivable. You stayed sane by spending the rest of your life trying to atone, trying to do enough good to make the pain tolerable. Today he'd do his best to find the con artist preying on the good people of Liberty.

Thankfully Theodora didn't pick up on his distress. "I spoke with your ex-wives this morning," she said. "They agreed to take half your pay by bank wire. They said they'd make sure your fiancé got a cut."

"*Ex*-fiancé. I make it a rule never to marry a woman who zeroes a gun on me."

"You think she would've fired?"

"I hope not." He mulled it over. "Maybe."

"You're doing right by her, that's all I can say. Some men wouldn't care about repaying a debt, although it's not really a debt. Anyone who puts cash in the stock market ought to have the sense to know they might lose their money. Of course, nowadays too many folks try to get rich without doing a lick of work. It's a modern madness." Theodora fired the Cadillac's engine. "If the trouble with Wish drags into next week, I'll send your women more cash." She grinned like Blackbeard. "*Ex*-women."

"I'm beginning to feel like an indentured servant." Not that he deserved any better. She pulled out of the lot, and he asked, "Where are we going?"

"You tell me."

Having her underfoot while he chased down leads wasn't sensible. "I thought I'd start at Bongo's Tavern, but I prefer to work alone. This morning one of the waitresses called in a tip."

"You've been bribing waitresses for information?"

"And barkeeps, maids in every hotel within thirty miles—why don't you drop me off at the car rental on Route 6? I was planning to stop there first. I can't do a decent job in the RV."

"I don't mind driving."

"And I don't want a partner. This is a man's job and you're . . . " Embarrassed, he shrugged.

"What? What am I?" Stomping down on the accelerator, she veered toward the center of the road. Not another car in sight but he instinctively thrust his right foot forward in search of an imaginary brake. "Get this through your thick skull, son. I'm not your partner. I'm your boss and one tough gal to boot. Save your gallantry for the next woman you marry."

"What's wrong with gallantry? Men should protect women."

"I don't need it."

She veered around a curve and he yelped. "Slow down!"

The Cadillac decreased in speed.

"Oh, Lordy. Are you one of those folks bedeviled by motion sickness?" Theodora asked with unexpected kindness. "Three of my grandkids have it. There's Dramamine in the glove box."

"I don't need Dramamine." He needed to work without having her tag along to slow progress.

"You think I can't hold my own in a tavern? Is that the boil growing on your butt?"

Her language was too colorful for his taste but it didn't change the facts. She was a mother, a grandmother—from what he'd heard, she had a few great-grandchildren too. If anything happened to her, how to explain to her family? "Bongo's isn't the proper place to take a lady," he said at last.

"You have a fine protective streak. Uncommon in men these days."

"I'll take that as a compliment." Probably the only one he'd receive from the feisty matriarch. "Theodora, from what Hugh has described, Bongo's is a rough joint. Drunks gather like fleas and a brawl is apt to break out at any moment. I never would've taken my mother to a dive and I won't take you."

Mention of his mother drew Theodora's attention, her expression opening like clouds parting to reveal the sun. "You loved her very much." It was a statement, not a question.

"I did."

"She's been gone a long time?"

"Nearly fifteen years, since my sophomore year in college." Heartache, pure and sharp, seized him. "She was a good woman." Reconsidering, he added, "She was the finest woman I've ever known, always putting everyone else's needs before her own, and a real optimist. Nothing got her down. If my sister had trouble with schoolwork or my football team lost a game, Mom could pull us out of a funk."

"Your father?"

"I hardly remember him. Liver cancer. It happened fast. Mom took over Dad's dry cleaning business, learned the books and hired two of my cousins part-time. I don't know how she got through those years. One of my cousins still runs the business."

The Cadillac drew to a stop at the light on County Line Road. The lonely acres of a farm had been recently tilled for spring planting. Miles ahead, the road seemed to drop off at the horizon.

The light changed, and Theodora sent the car forward with a jerky start. "Your sister still lives in Philadelphia?"

"Accountant. Greeks stick together, and she does

tax work for most of the small businesses in our neighborhood." He couldn't bear to describe Calista. Bright, strong, the one person in the world who had every reason to despise him. Yet she'd always been his greatest champion. "She's done well for herself."

"She sounds like a good girl."

"She is."

A garish sign appeared in the distance. They'd reached their destination.

He was about to speak when Theodora said, "Son, I lived through the Cold War and the Civil Rights Movement. I can hold my own in a tavern."

It was probably the truth, but he had no intention of testing the theory. He got out quickly.

She tried to follow but he pushed the driver door shut. "I'm begging you," he said in his most persuasive voice. "Stay in the car. I can't in good conscience escort an elderly woman through a bar as rundown as this one. I might not be able to protect you."

Her shoulders twitched. "No one tells me what to do."

He surveyed the line of motorcycles parked before the tavern. Near them a drunk wove a zigzag path toward the woods in back, probably to take a piss. "Just stay in the car. This will only take a minute."

He left her sputtering at his retreating back.

As promised, the waitress who'd called in the tip was seated in a booth up front.

A group of bikers milled around the tables in back. Evidently none of the patrons cared about imbibing before noon or Ohio's No Smoking law. The place reeked of tobacco and boozy *joie de vivre.* The heavyset waitress stubbed out a butt as Hector slid into the seat opposite.

She got right to it. "The guys I called you about? Last night they were here for a couple hours." The woman fiddled with her cheap hoop earrings before continuing.

112

"They aren't locals—I've never seen them before. I'm pretty sure they stole the tip jar on their way out."

"Can you describe them?"

"They were mean bastards. They reminded me of weasels—small eyes and weak chins. Skinny too, but all muscle. They had a look that scared me, like they'd drown kittens for sport." The woman pulled her hands into her lap. "All the local guys steered clear of them."

From the description, he doubted either was Wish dressed in one of her famous disguises. Even in costume, she couldn't hide her sex appeal. The men she impersonated were usually attractive, not weasels.

"Was it just the two of them?" he asked. He had no idea if they worked for her but hoped to hear of a third accomplice.

"For most of the night," she replied, drawing his sharp regard. "Right before closing a guy came in to get them. He snapped his fingers and they got right up, like they were scared of him or something."

The hairs on the back of Hector's neck stood at attention.

Wish.

"The guy who came in, what did he look like?"

"Long hair, mustache—he was dressed like a middle-aged hippie. Kind of good-looking. But he was mean like his friends. He looked at me like I was something nasty squashed on the heel of his boot." Her face fell. "I noticed the tip jar missing right after they left."

He pitied the woman. The bags beneath her eyes were ashen, the broken tooth at the front of her mouth in dire need of a cap.

"How much did you lose?" he asked.

"Seventeen dollars and twenty-five cents."

"That's a lot." It wasn't by his measure. But different people had different yardsticks.

"You're telling me. Half the night's tips."

He threw a twenty on the table. "For your time." She started to thank him but he jumped in, adding, "If they come back, call me immediately. Don't wait, okay? I need to catch them while they're here."

"I'm sorry. Long shift, and I forgot where I put your—"

The words died on her lips. Her eyes rounded.

Sunlight cut across the floor.

A man's gravelly laugh entered from the parking lot, followed by a higher male voice joining in. Hector glanced over his shoulder, his senses on high alert and his ears buzzing with the slow motion tension he recalled from his military service in Iraq.

The joviality the two men shared was snuffed out as they picked up on the danger, their eyes lifting. They looked at the waitress then back at the door.

Hector lunged.

The taller man launched outside, throwing the door wide to spill the sun's glare into the tavern. Half-blinded, Hector got the smaller man in his sights. He caught the bastard around the waist, plowing him into the wall. The waitress screamed. A shelf loaded with shot glasses collapsed with a *BOOM*, startling everyone in the place. The man wrenched free.

By the time he'd dashed halfway across the parking lot, his accomplice was inside a late model Honda. The car peeled from the lot.

Abandoned, the second man wheeled in a desperate circle. His moment of indecision gave hope, and Hector's muscles burned as he took chase, catapulting across the gravel on an angry growl. The man swung toward the woods. Hector dived headfirst, hurtling them both to the ground. The impact sent stars spinning through his vision.

They rolled across the gravel but he managed to land a punch on the man's jaw. The guy was mostly bones and sinew but he possessed surprising strength, holding off another strike by landing one of his own in Hector's ribs. The impact sent another band of stars through Hector's vision. Pain sliced through his gut. They rolled to a stop but the man was still swinging with fierce precision, his fists landing painful strikes on Hector's cheek, shoulder, eyes.

From above, Theodora's voice was dangerously low. "Hit him again, and I'll put a bullet in your brain," she growled.

The man's fist froze in midair. Sputtering, Hector tried to clear his vision. The blackness retreating, he choked out a breath.

Theodora pressed the barrel of the Winchester rifle into the man's cheek. His eyes rolled in their sockets as he tried to fix on the danger. She pressed harder, drawing a whimper.

"Stop whining, you fool." To Hector, flat on his back staring open-mouthed, she said, "Snap out of it, son. Are you going to lie there all day or help me haul this scoundrel to the police?"

Chapter 8

A few stragglers were finishing breakfast at The Second Chance Grill. At a table near the counter, Snoops was tooling around on her laptop.

Given the ordeal she'd undergone, she looked remarkably fit. The yellowish bruises on her cheeks were fading and her eyes were bright. Although her right leg was encased in a cast, she appeared on the mend.

Birdie placed her hands on her hips in mock disapproval. "Something is wrong with this picture. Where's your best friend?" Snoops and Blossom were inseparable. It was rare to find one without the other.

"It's not the weekend, silly. Where do you think she is?"

"Oh. Right."

Snoops pointed at her cast. *"This* got me a free pass. I go back to school tomorrow. Since my parents are at work, Ethel Lynn said it's all right if I stick around until Blossom shows up. Plus she said it's okay if I eat tons of ice cream while I wait."

Ice cream wasn't a palatable breakfast food but then, adolescents were from a different planet. "Nice deal," she said. "Are you in much pain?"

"It comes and goes." Nervously the girl tapped her purple-framed glasses. "Everyone says it was your mom driving your car. She looked just like a man with a mustache and messy hair. She really *is* a mistress of disguise."

"One of her many talents."

Snoops grimaced the way she might if she tasted bitter fruit. "The YouTube video of your car going off the cliff is getting lots of shares on Twitter and Facebook. Blossom says everyone in the junior high has seen it—even the teachers."

Losing the car was no picnic, but it didn't compare to what had happened to Snoops. "Twenty minutes of fame thanks to my mother's vindictive streak," she said. "As far as I'm concerned, I'd let her total twenty cars if it meant she wouldn't play chicken with you on your bike."

The comment's sincerity pleased Snoops. "I don't think she was trying to hit me," she replied. She sent a sweet glance. "She probably thought she'd freak me out by following too close. I didn't see the ditch by the road. It was my fault I fell."

"Nothing is your fault." Birdie cradled the girl's cheek. "My mother had no right driving so close. It was irresponsible."

"It *was* kind of stupid."

Another sweet glance, and Birdie couldn't resist planting a kiss on the girl's brow. She smelled of honey and ginger, her skin soft. The anger Birdie had managed to hold at bay rushed in, followed by the horror at the prospect of what might have occurred. What if the bicycle had gone under the Vette instead of catapulting down the embankment? What if her mother's senseless actions had caused Snoops' death?

"I'm so sorry you were hurt. If I'd known my mother would go after you, I would've done anything to stop her."

"It's okay. Honest."

"It's never okay for an adult to put a child in danger. It's inexcusable."

"Sure. I get that, but I'm the one who owes *you* an apology."

"I can't imagine why."

Snoops was one of the nicest kids in Liberty. Worse case scenario, she'd accidently deleted some of the newspaper's files during an install. Wouldn't be the first time.

"You don't understand. See, I'm really smart." Defiance sparked the girl's eyes. "I should've thought of something by now. I just can't think of a way to find your mom. I'm good with puzzles, but this one has me stumped."

"Keep your chin up. We'll think of something." She surveyed the dining room. "Where is everyone?"

"You mean Delia and Ethel Lynn? They're in the kitchen. Something happened, but they're being real secretive." Worry clouded Snoops' black bean eyes. "I think Finney's crying."

Finney, crying?

The cook was as tough as leather baking in the sun. She had a temper as hot as July and the disposition of a bulldog. It was difficult to imagine anything penetrating her tough exterior.

During last winter's blizzard a woman in Ethel Lynn's knitting circle had suffered a stroke and died. Finney was the only woman in Liberty not blubbering into a handkerchief. Many of the circle's members were widows, and the stoic cook put chains on the tires of her truck to ferry them to the church service and the graveside memorial, Ethel Lynn included. Finney didn't witness much of either event, her brassy hair stiff with frost as she braved the frigid temperatures and played chauffeur for more than a dozen women.

Now, in the restaurant's kitchen, the mood seemed to mark an equally somber occasion. Ethel Lynn and Delia huddled together like helpless onlookers. Dr. Mary Chance, dressed in her white physician's coat, stood over the cook who was, unbelievably, sobbing in a chair by the stove.

Mary's family practice was located on the second floor of the building, right above the restaurant. The doctor was just a few years younger than Birdie with warm, mossy green eyes and chestnut hair. Although she'd been married to Anthony Perini for less than a year, she'd already formed a tight bond with his daughter Blossom. Mary was Liberty's only local doctor, a soft-spoken woman Birdie admired.

Clearly the situation was serious if Mary had left her patients to come downstairs, even if only for a few minutes. She was stroking Finney's hair and murmuring in her ear. The cook, hunched forward to hide her face, howled into her splayed hands.

Ethel Lynn, quivering by the sink, noticed Birdie. "We don't know why she's overwrought," she said before a question was brought forth. "The police were here. The minute they left, she fell to pieces."

"The police came to see Finney?" Apprehension took the moisture from Birdie's mouth. Wish had caused more trouble. She was sure of it. This time she'd hurt Finney.

"They were only here for a moment," Ethel Lynn said. "A call came in about gunplay at Bongo's and they left."

Delia popped a stick of gum into her mouth. "Are you sure you heard right? Lots of bikers hang out at Bongo's but most of those guys are harmless."

"I know what I heard! Emmeline Fisher, the girl on dispatch? She got all frazzled and blurted it out. Someone called the police station to report guns drawn in the parking lot."

120

"Was anyone shot?" Delia asked, her disbelief replaced with concern.

"Heavens, I hope not," Ethel Lynn said, picking at the lacy cuff of her blue sateen dress. If she didn't stop soon, she'd unravel the threads. "The police wouldn't give details. The call came in and they high-tailed it out of here."

Finney's sobs lessened. From over her head, Mary caught Birdie's attention. "A glass of water," Mary said, her composure unruffled by the discussion of violence at the tavern.

Birdie rushed to do her bidding, filling a glass with cold water. Mary urged Finney to take a sip between hiccupping sobs. The cook's eyes were swollen from so much crying, her nose runny. Birdie spotted the box of tissues by the sink and carried it over.

The cook withdrew three tissues in quick succession, her wrist snapping sharply. This small evidence of her spirits rebounding was a welcome sight. Sorrow was a stupefying emotion, rendering its host too muddled to attack a problem. Anger led to action, and if Wish had in some way harmed the cook, they had to do something about it.

Birdie still loved her mother with the weary devotion that came from being the child of a criminal, the allegiance long frayed by Wish's exploits and cruelty. But she loved Finney more, loved the way she planted her overlarge feet when making a point and stuck her neck out to help friends and acquaintances alike. If this were a choice between broken affection and love sure to endure, she'd choose Finney because the cook—through numerous acts of kindness and brusque offerings of advice—had demonstrated time and again she'd always choose Birdie.

Mary also noticed the change in the cook's state of mind. She laid her hands on Finney's shoulders, lending her the strength to proceed.

Finney nearly collapsed into another bout of tears, a gargled cry rising from her throat. Somehow she drew on an inner well of strength and straightened her spine.

"Wish had on one of her disguises," she said, rubbing her eyes. "My children let her right in. They believed her nonsense about installing free Internet. They let her right into my house and asked if she'd lock up when she left!"

Mary, who knew Finney better than anyone, said, "Don't be too hard on your kids. How were they to know they'd let a thief into the house?"

"They should've known. Yesterday Hugh ran an article in the *Liberty Post* warning folks to be on the lookout. Half the stores on The Square have cash missing from the till and customers complaining about pick pockets. The only reason The Second Chance hasn't been hit is because we've been vigilant. My kids should've known better."

Mary was having none of it. "The restaurant has been lucky," she said reasonably. "Finney, I have new patients coming into my practice every week. You may think you know everyone in town, but that isn't the point. I now have patients from Bellrywood and other nearby towns—you don't know all their faces. If Wish puts on one of her disguises and decides to rob The Second Chance, I doubt any of us can stop her."

"Maybe so. Even in a small town, I can't know everyone. Especially not with your practice growing the way it is. With new people coming in, and transients increasing, strangers don't stick out like they used to. But that doesn't excuse my kids. They don't have an ounce of brains between them."

Softly, Birdie said, "They're teenagers. Cut them some slack." She wanted to protect Randy and Marla from their mother's wrath nearly as much as she dreaded learning what had been stolen. "Kids don't read the newspaper."

Finney was unconvinced. "Snoops does. She reads the *Post* and *The Economist* too. Strangest thing I ever saw. Why would a girl in junior high care about the world economy? There's nothing with ink the girl won't read. "

Despite the seriousness of the situation, Birdie grinned. "Snoops isn't typical. She's smarter than all of us combined." On a more somber note, she added, "Most of the adults in Liberty are shielding their kids from hearing about what's happening. Blossom and Snoops know, but only because they're involved. Even the kids in Snoops' classes are in the dark about her accident—she's telling friends she took a bad tumble off her bike."

"Say what you like. It doesn't excuse my Randy and Marla. They're nearly grown. They know better than to leave a stranger alone in the house. I'm grounding them for life."

"If you do, my mother has won," Birdie said, her voice severe. The comment got the cook's attention, and she added, "Don't you see? She could've broken in while you were at work, and Randy and Marla were at school. She had more than enough time. But she didn't. Think about it, Finney. *Why* did she enter while your teenagers were at home?"

This finally sank in.

Rising on unsteady legs, Finney looked past Birdie's shoulder, the ruddy color in her cheeks seeping away as her mind worked overtime. When she'd worked it all out, she said, "Wish knew my kids were home. She planned to rob me *when* they were home. She knew I'd come down hard on them."

"It's not enough to thrust the knife in. She likes to twist it." Holding the cook's gaze was unbearable, and Birdie lowered her eyes. "I'll bet she followed you to learn your schedule. She tailed you, and another lowlife followed Randy and Marla. She had the whole thing mapped out."

"Then it's true," Ethel Lynn interjected. "She's not working alone."

"Probably not."

Finney sent a savage look. "And she wants me to punish Randy and Marla?" she asked. "My poor defenseless children?" The cook sent a dark look Birdie's way. "No offense, Birdie—when I get my hands on her, I'm stringing her up by the short hairs. I'll follow up by knocking her out cold with my skillet."

It was clear she wasn't serious and the comment relieved some of the tension in the kitchen. "Not to worry," Birdie said, offering a weary smile. "I'll help string her up. I'd rather you didn't knock her out cold. She deserves your wrath but she *is* my mother."

Mary, glancing swiftly at her watch, got to the point they were all avoiding. "Finney, what exactly did Wish take?"

The question drove the cook back into the chair. The courage she'd packed in her spine melted away.

"How much?" Mary prodded.

"Six thousand four hundred and twenty-eight dollars."

All of the women stared, aghast, but Ethel Lynn had the strongest reaction. The dizzying sum was like a strong wind knocking her back against the sink.

"Egads! What were you doing with so much money in the house?" She cradled her skull, the lace at her wrists flapping. "Thousands of dollars—gone!"

"Shut up already. You aren't making me feel better."

"Why should you? Thousands! I think I'll be sick."

"Old woman, if you upchuck on my kitchen floor it'll be your last foolishness for all eternity."

Birdie took a tentative step closer. "Why *did* you have so much cash in the house?" she asked.

The question fused the cook's brows in a line of disgust. "Remember the Wall Street meltdown? After

Lehmann Brothers went belly up and half the mortgages in the country looked dodgy?"

"Sure." She didn't remember much. At the time she'd been a pickpocket roaming the country, and didn't have savings much less money invested in stocks.

"I lost nearly half of my retirement during the mess. All that saving and squirrelling money away just to have it go up in smoke. After, well, I thought I'd keep some of my cash out of banks. Just to be safe."

Mary shook her head with bemusement. "The Great Depression revisited. Please tell me you did *not* have the money stuffed beneath your mattress."

Finney rolled her head sideways, glanced up at Mary, then began picking at her nails.

"I don't believe it." Mary patted her on the back. "Shake off your blues. Since I'm the proud owner of this establishment, I think it's time to give you a raise. I'm doubling your salary, effective immediately."

"Stop your nonsense. I'm not having my salary doubled, not like this."

"I insist."

Mary's offer was nice, but Birdie knew it wasn't logical. Recently wed, with a medical practice she was still getting off the ground—how would she manage? Her husband Anthony owned the Gas & Go across The Square, and they were still paying medical bills after Blossom's hard-won victory over leukemia. The Second Chance Grill enjoyed decent profits, but not enough to warrant doubling the cook's salary.

"I have a better idea," Birdie said. Fishing around her purse, she found her checkbook. "Finney, I'm paying you back. My mother stole your money. It's only right that I return every dime. I'm just sick about what she did to Snoops, the town and now you."

She was still searching for a pen when Finney got into her face. Nose to nose, she said, "Birdie Kaminsky, sometimes you're as dumb as mud. What makes you think I need your charity? It's not like you robbed my house, and I know you don't control your mother. The only thing sure to control her is a pair of handcuffs." Pulling her chin tight to her neck, she took in Birdie's knit top and jeans with a look veering from surprise to approval. "What happened to your fancy clothes? Those leather mini-skirts that showed off your ass and those silky blouses? This is the first time I've seen you dressed sensibly since those rubies made you rich."

Birdie tried to duck away from the cook's glittering stare. Her feet were glued to the floor. "Hector told me to tone it down, at least until my mother leaves."

"He did, did he? I like Hector." Rocking back on her heels, Finney asked, "How much of your inheritance have you wasted on silk and leather?"

"More than my mother stole from you if that's what you're driving at." More than double, really—she'd recklessly run through thousands. What had Hugh said on the day he'd walked out?

You're trying to fill a hole in your heart with expensive baubles and trips to the mall. Maybe you can't feel contentment because it's outside your emotional repertoire.

The lesson he'd tried to teach was reflected in Finney's eyes. "If you're in the mood to do charity, try giving some to yourself," she said. "Forget about the money you've inherited. Leave it be, like Theodora and her kin have done for generations. They work hard, Birdie, and they live within their means. A woman born a slave carried those rubies all the way to Ohio, and she was a sight more honorable than all of us. Justice Postell was born a slave, but she walked her way to freedom. You'll never be half as free until you earn your own way in the world."

Beside him on the couch in the police chief's office,

Hector's pint-sized savior was drawn into herself like a caterpillar wrapped in a cocoon.

In retrospect her heroism at Bongo's Tavern was remarkable. Hector had been nearly beaten unconscious but she'd moved like lightning, grabbing her Winchester rifle—a gun nearly matching her in height—from the trunk of her Cadillac to save him. She'd loaded and cocked the rifle in a flash.

His head still throbbed from the beating he'd received. The assailant and suspected accomplice of Wish Kaminsky was now in a holding cell being questioned by Chief Clay Burnes and two of his officers. Hector had brushed off the chief's offer of a ride to the hospital. Nothing was broken but his pride after receiving a whipping from a man barely in his twenties and a good head shorter in height.

A secretary with a nose like a beacon waddled into the room with a teacup and saucer. She set it down before Theodora and quietly left. Under normal circumstances Hector would find china with a rosebud pattern a strange addition to the guns and ammo stored at a police station. But this was Liberty, and he suspected it was kept on hand for the chief's female guests. With the danger now past, Theodora was shaken up badly. The hot tea would do her good.

The perfumed scent rising from the cup rousted her from her stupor. She curled her fingers around the cup's delicate handle, the saucer rattling with the effort.

"Let me help," he said, taking the cup and holding it to her lips. The muscles surrounding her jaw twitched. Feeling sympathetic given her reaction, and more than a little grateful for her courage, he added, "Some day we're having, isn't it? Gunplay before lunch. It's not my idea of fun. That's right, sip the tea slowly. You'll feel better."

"I'm fine," she said between sips, and he was grateful for the gravelly sound of her voice. Like him, she'd refused a visit to the hospital. Only she'd done so with more gusto, threatening to get her rifle from the car if the officers and their staff didn't stop fussing over her. "Compared to you, I'm in great shape."

"That isn't saying much."

"It is from where I'm sitting." Her gaze hopped across his face assessing the damage. He caught the tenderness in her eyes and a playful look that, for a fraction of a second, made her look decades younger. "You're getting a shiner. Mean one, too."

"A small battle wound. It'll heal in no time."

Her eyes twinkled like dark gems. "You moved like a farmhand wrestling a muddy pig to the ground. I enjoyed the show."

"Thanks. I don't know about muddy livestock, but I'm glad he's in lock-up."

Chief Burnes came in. He was a barrel-chested man with the erect posture of someone who'd seen military duty in his youth. He had a thatch of hair the color of toast and a thoughtful, nearly genteel demeanor. Pausing before the couch where he'd insisted Theodora wait while he dealt with the prisoner, he seemed reluctant to share whatever information he'd gathered.

Edgy, Theodora appraised him. "Spit it out, Clay. What have you found out?"

Like everyone else in Liberty, he seemed in possession of unlimited patience when it came to Theodora. Wheeling his chair out from behind his desk, he sat knee to knee with her. There was something touching about his deference to Liberty's grand matriarch, and he spoke to her in a soothing way that reduced the trembling in her hands.

"His name is Willet Pearson, last known address in Houston," the chief said. "He's been off the grid for two years—Houston PD got a tip he'd gone to Mexico. Not much on his rap sheet, other than breaking and entering at age nineteen and car theft two years earlier. He's suspected in a dozen crimes in Texas and Arkansas."

She *harrumphed* with disapproval. "Your typical ruffian. The other crimes—mostly the pickpocket variety?"

"For the most part. He usually works with his older brother James, also suspected of crossing the Rio Grande two years ago."

"Is the older brother in Liberty?"

"I would imagine. They're inseparable. James is probably the man who left the scene at Bongo's in the late model Honda. We don't have a license plate but we're looking for the car."

Hector asked, "What has Willet Pearson told you about Wish?"

The question sent the chief's worried glance to Theodora. "I think he knows we don't have much on him, other than the altercation outside Bongo's. As for Kaminsky, he says he doesn't know her. He's not doing much talking at all."

The denial wasn't much of a surprise, and Hector knew they'd never tie the bastard to Wish without proof. "How long can you hold him?" he asked.

"Twenty-four hours. We've charged him with assault, but he can make bail."

"That's it? What about the complaints from the stores on The Square? The residents in town complaining about a pickpocket?"

"We're also investigating the robbery of Finney Smith's house," the chief said with frustration. At Theodora's questioning look he added, "We can't hold Pearson for crimes we suspect he committed, or helped the Kaminsky woman commit. Not without proof. If he's involved in any of those crimes, he worked in disguise. Maybe a variety of disguises. We put him in a line-up but none of the shop owners identified him as the thief."

"Wish taught him well," Theodora muttered. She

129

curled back into herself.

She seemed content to let the men talk, and Hector said, "So he walks out of here on bail. Then what?"

"I'll have a cruiser tail him, but it won't do much good. I don't have the manpower to put an officer on Pearson twenty-four/seven."

"Meaning he'll be back in business with Wish by tomorrow?" It seemed they'd never catch a break.

"Possibly. We'll keep questioning him. Maybe it'll scare him into leaving town as soon as he's released. Can't say I like bail jumpers, but if he takes his brother with him, I *will* rest easier."

"Don't count on it. Wish will bribe them both into staying until she's ready to blow out of here."

"I hate to agree. Hopefully we'll catch her in the commission of a crime. Every criminal's luck runs out eventually."

Hugh came in. He looked harried with his hair sticking out in all directions and his tie undone. His attention skimmed Theodora before moving to Hector with an odd curiosity, as if seeing him for the first time and taking his measure, man to man. Hector grew uneasy beneath the tight appraisal.

After an interminable moment, Liberty's lead reporter severed the connection. "Have you found Wish?" he asked the chief.

By the time he was brought up to speed, Theodora had closed her eyes. She'd experienced too many shocks today, more than a woman her age could endure. Reflecting on her actions, Hector's admiration for her grew.

"We need to get you home," he said to her gently. "You've already given a statement. There's nothing more you can do."

Chief Burnes nodded in agreement. "He's right, Theodora. You might as well go on home. I'll call you with updates."

130

With her eyelids still closed, Theodora said, "Why don't you good-for-nothings stop badgering about me and get a plan together? It's time you hunted down the mistress of disguise. Go on, all of you. I'll drive myself in a moment."

They left her in peace. In the corridor, Hugh stopped Hector. "We need to talk," Hugh said.

"Then talk." Hector wasn't sure why he suddenly felt defensive, but whatever it was bothering the reporter, it seemed serious.

"Not here."

"Why not?"

Hugh produced his car keys, his gaze dancing across the floor with the rapidity of his thoughts.

It *was* serious. On a frown, Hector followed him out of the station.

Chapter 9

Finny's harsh advice accompanied Birdie out of The Second Chance Grill and all the way to practically nowhere given how far she'd walked.

Many of Liberty's tree-lined streets were familiar, the close-knit neighborhoods with kids' bicycles flung across lawns and couples sipping tea on front porches swathed in dappled shade.

The streets extended from the nexus of Liberty Square like the arms of a starfish, the pretty shops at the town's hub giving way to wealthier neighborhoods that boasted Gothic mansions of golden stone and rambling Colonials with spring tulips bursting from well-tended flowerbeds. But those streets were now behind her, mostly ignored and unappreciated as the memory of the conversation she'd shared with Finney at The Second Chance carried her further, over railroad tracks and past a small convenience store. Her heart was bruised and her thoughts cluttered after the blunt advice she'd received from the cook.

An odd sensation darted through her, and she looked around quickly to ensure she wasn't being followed. A car sped past, the three children in the backseat shouting something at their harried mother. No other cars, and the street was void of pedestrians. Shrugging off the sensation, Birdie paused to take note of her surroundings.

She wasn't familiar with this quiet cul-de-sac at the town's southern end and a good two miles from The Square. A neighborhood of working-class families, the houses snuggled close as if in defense of harsh economic times. There were no lavish displays of tulips here, and more than one house needed a fresh coat of paint. On the front stoop of one bungalow, a snowy-haired man sat gazing at the clouds.

He acknowledged her with a jaunty tip of his head as she strode past. It was probably close to 3 P.M. and time to return to the *Post,* although she didn't have copy to write or articles to edit. Without fanfare Hugh had handed off most of her workload to the newbies he'd hired, allowing her to do whatever she wanted, which meant, given her state of mind, she wasn't doing much at all.

If her lack of motivation wasn't enough to stir the guilt, she now had Finney's comments ringing through her head like the disagreeable sounds of an early morning alarm.

The offer she'd made to cover the cook's losses had been a goodwill gesture. It seemed the right thing to do after Wish robbed Finney of her hard-earned savings. Losing over six thousand dollars—the loss represented several month's pay, a fortune to a single mother raising two kids. If Birdie's offer came across as misguided charity, the insult wasn't intentional.

She loved Finney and would never purposely hurt her.

Now, after walking for miles in deep reflection, she still didn't understand what the cook meant about giving charity to herself before offering it to others. The comment was as puzzling as it was vexing.

Trying to work it out, she wondered if kindness

134

was the root of all charity.

Weren't people with kind natures considerate and generous, and more apt to lend a hand than push you out of the way in pursuit of a prize? They possessed an abundance of sympathy—and empathy.

With regard to how she treated herself, Birdie knew those traits didn't come easily. When it came to feeding her own soul, she was a miser. If Hugh nagged and prodded, his rebukes were mild compared to the chastisement she heaped on herself during the naked hours before dawn when she woke from nightmares or during the day, alone in her car, mired in thought. There was no banishing the small, insidious voice that doubted every good deed or attempt at improvement. She didn't think she was good enough or smart enough—or deserving.

Never did she practice a quiet encouragement during the dialogue she conducted in her head, or hope for something other than failure. Which had everything to do with self-worth. Or, in her case, a lack of it.

The final house in the cul-de-sac was now behind her.

She spied a white clapboard church set back from the street's curving sidewalk. The church wasn't much larger than the residences clustered around its perimeter but the cross at its pitch was pretty, a gleaming patch of gold catching sunbeams.

Around the building's foundation, marigolds marched in a cheerful line. The wooden steps leading to the open double doors were dressed with ceramic pots of yellow and purple pansies.

On a whim, she went inside.

The nave rested beneath a pleasing silence. No one in sight, and she slid into a pew midway up the aisle. A mouthwatering aroma carried on the air and it took a moment for the scent to register—cinnamon. The aroma increased in intensity, setting her stomach to rumbling, and she wondered if cinnamon rolls were coming out of an oven somewhere on the church grounds.

Did the pastor and his family live nearby, perhaps in a house out back?

It was easy enough to imagine a plain-faced brood with big hearts and simple ways, the wife spilling flour and sugar across the kitchen, the two children hopping off the school bus and dashing inside to pour glasses of cold milk and wait, panting, for the latest confectionary delight to appear beneath their noses.

In the evenings the family played board games together and shared the small treasures of their day. The children rose early on Saturdays to sweep the nave's wooden floor and water the flowers outside before skipping down the street to play with friends.

A boy and a girl, she imagined, twins would be nice, and they were careful when approaching the linen draped altar at the head of the chancel, or when tiptoeing past the podium, where their father sent inspiring words over the heads of his flock on Sundays.

Caught by her musings, she wondered if she had it all wrong. Grinning, she shook her head. Put her and Hugh in the imaginary roles of the parents and *he* would be the one whipping up tantalizing meals in the kitchen. Not that she could imagine herself in the place of the minister— crowds frightened her, and she didn't have the wisdom to lead anyone. It would be a miracle if she ever got her own life in order.

Yet the daydream soothed her spirits with its simple design of goodness in the town she'd grown to love. Inspired by it, she stretched her neck to hunt for the donation box. Maybe charity *did* begin with herself—she'd have to work on that—but what was the sin in helping others? A church serving a working class neighborhood would appreciate her gift.

She noticed a wooden box attached to the wall by the door where she'd entered. Quickly she wrote the check and dropped it inside.

The check had barely released from her fingertips when a shadow fell across the nave's floor. A terrible knowing stole the moisture from her mouth.

"My, aren't you a do-gooder."

The voice, husky and horribly familiar, lifted Birdie's gaze.

The photograph blinked on Hugh's laptop like a taunt. Hector gave only a cursory glance before averting his eyes.

"Why were you looking into my past?" he asked, although the answer was easy to deduce. Hugh was a reporter. The need to ferret out the truth was an ingrained habit. Plus he didn't like Hector flirting with Birdie, a habit just as deeply rooted if, for the most part, innocent.

For their private chat Hugh had chosen a bench near the granite steps rising into the county courthouse on Liberty Square. At the top of the steps, a police officer strolled back and forth in the spring air. Did Hugh choose the location in case he needed backup if Hector took a swing?

It wouldn't happen.

"Your ex-wives . . . how are they now?" On the laptop Hugh pulled up a second photo and positioned it beside the first.

Resisting, Hector crossed his ankles. Sparks of anger invaded his line of vision but he fought them down.

"I'm just asking," Hugh said. "Are they fine now?"

"They're great."

"Must've been tough going. For them, and you."

"It was."

Hugh let the silence lengthen. He seemed content to

137

wait until Hector stopped brooding and started talking. At last Hector said, "My first wife, Sil? She had three years of therapy and two surgeries. It was rough."

"It sounds like it."

"I found her a yoga instructor to teach her basic poses and meditation. Sure beat living zonked out on pain meds." Downward Dog and Child's Pose—yoga was one of those last-ditch efforts that reaped incredible benefits. "Sil's been hooked on yoga ever since. Seriously, she's turned her body into a rubber band. She can bend in ways that shouldn't be humanly possible."

"And Bunny?" Hugh smiled encouragingly.

"Luckier. Two years of rehab, no surgery. After we divorced, she took a job at The University of Virginia."

"Professor?"

"Librarian. These days, she runs in the Boston Marathon. Never misses it."

"You're still friends with them both." A statement not a question, and he caught a note of admiration in the words.

"Great friends, if you leave out how I invested their money in the wrong stocks," Hector said. "Can't say either one's happy about my stupidity. Doesn't seem to matter. They still look out for me. They *like* to look out for me, if you can believe it."

"Count your blessings. Before I met Birdie, every woman crazy enough to live with me took something on her way out. My big screen TV, stereo—they always had a thing for electronics. Not that I blame them for using a blunt spoon to dig speakers out of my walls. I'd never commit to making a relationship long-term. Funny how that pisses women off."

Hector looked at Hugh squarely. "And now you have, with Birdie," he said, glad to escape the spotlight. "Made a real commitment, I mean."

"I hope so. The jury's still out on if she'll settle

down," Hugh replied, and the admiration in his voice gave way to doubt. "We got engaged too fast. I should've done a better job getting her used to the idea."

"You mean you should've worn her down, bit by bit."

"Basically."

The clichés about women wanting to settle down and men wanting to roam free weren't entirely accurate, at least not for him or, from the looks of it, Hugh. What was better than finding the right woman, someone to share the best and worst life offered?

Monogamy sure beat one-night stands with women draped across barstools, the young party animals and their older, more cynical brethren. Plus there was the bit about fatherhood, a status Hector hoped to claim someday. He liked most of what he knew about children, especially the dreamy phase he thought of as Little Land when kids believed in everything from the tooth fairy to Santa Claus. Maybe the teenage years took stamina but from what he'd seen, most parents made it through without losing their hair or their sanity.

"I could give you pointers, at least on how to get a woman to the altar," he said. "Getting a woman to stay? I've got nothing."

"I don't either." Ruefully Hugh shook his head. "If I find a way to keep Birdie, I'll let you in on the secret."

"Pal, they're *all* different. Most men share at least some comparable traits, but women? No two are alike. They come with an emotional range way beyond us and twice the smarts."

"Amen."

Cowardice wasn't a trait worth cultivating, and Hector knew he'd delayed long enough. He looked at the images blinking on the laptop.

The similarities between the wedding photographs were readily apparent. In both, the bride and groom sent big smiles at the camera. A different bride each time and two images of Hector taken five years apart in the same black tuxedo with the same triumphant expression on his face. And he *had* been happy if not head over heels for Sil, dressed elegantly in an ivory gown, and Bunny, who'd gone overboard with her fluffy concoction of white chiffon and lace.

Each bride was seated in a wheelchair.

On the day they'd wed, it hadn't been clear if either would walk again. Hector hadn't worried too much, mostly because he was a born and bred optimist. He said his vows intent on seeing each of his wives through the trials and frustrations of physical therapy, the crying jags and moments of rage. Even when each woman tried to give up, he refused. And both *had* walked again.

"You can understand my curiosity about your life," Hugh was saying. "You've become important to Theodora—and Birdie. The resume you sent for the bounty hunter job was adequate but like all resumes, it didn't have much in the way of personal details. Then I dug deeper and found the police report about your sister's accident."

The sympathy rimming his words was unbearable. Hector despised it nearly as much as he despised his inability to block the memory's assault. Not of his wives. These days, Sil and Bunny were past the tragedy they'd suffered.

It was the other memory, the one that led a broken young man in to two wrong marriages, now bearing down on him.

The night before coming home to his mother and sister, he'd partied late at the frat house, a raucous celebration before the University of Pennsylvania student body went on break for Thanksgiving holiday. The next afternoon he'd been nursing a hangover on Mom's couch when the blast of sound shook through the house clear down to the foundation, an awful din of grinding metal and

140

exploding glass.

Later, at the hospital, he sobbed like a beaten child when he learned the facts. The drunk had swerved onto the street at a deadly 60 mph.

Initially, during the ear-curdling blast destined to change his life, Hector experienced an unnerving surprise. He wasn't sure how long it took to shake off the sleepiness and the last fragments of the hangover, but he'd done so by the time the shrill cries of an ambulance reached him.

Denial followed him across the living room. With it came a ridiculous hope. Surely the first sound was imagined and he'd go outside to find yet another ambulance ferrying a woman to hospital to deliver a baby or transport a guy having a coronary—a typical disturbance in the festering hive of humanity he'd escaped with the scholarship to Penn.

But the ambulance didn't pass.

It stopped three doors down, the paramedics leaping out amid the shattered glass and twisted steel. The street looked like a bomb had gone off. The air smelled of engine oil and a woman, on the sidewalk, was screaming.

His mother, unconscious, was flung over the Buick's steering wheel. She'd bleed out before the paramedics reached her, another excruciating truth Hector wouldn't learn until later.

He rushed outside. Seeing what lay in the road, his knees gave out. On all fours, he vomited.

The impact of the drunk driver's pickup had thrown his sister through the front window of his mother's car. Calista was face down in the street in a grotesque posture.

The memory fled as Hugh, in an act of mercy, placed a hand on Hector's shoulder. Hector jumped like he'd been touched by fire.

Hugh backed off. "I didn't mean to upset you."

If this was an apology, it did nothing to alleviate the

141

grief swarming in his gut. "So you know," Hector said. "Congratulations."

"Man, I'm sorry."

"You should be." With focus, he kept the memory from reaching back inside him. It was a trick he'd learned, like the meditative breathing Sil used to ward off pain. "Just give me some space."

"Whatever you need." Hugh looked across the green, at a group of kids kicking around a soccer ball. "I think I've misjudged you."

"No kidding."

"Why *did* you marry them?"

"Sil and Bunny?" Thankfully he hadn't mentioned Calista, at least not yet. "It wasn't like I went looking for women dealing with handicaps. Sometimes you run into someone and . . . I don't know, you click. We hit it off."

"Sure. They were nice women."

"I didn't care about the wheelchair. I liked them for who they were, maybe for how much they wanted to get better, walk again."

A frothy irritation churned inside him. It took some doing, but Hector found his bearings. This wasn't a criticism—Hugh had a genuine interest in learning why an able-bodied man wed two women in a row, both injured by drunk drivers. Life was full of random events; you made choices without much thought of the reasons behind them. The logic of how something happened, or why, wasn't apparent until years later. As it was now.

"I was at fault for the accident, the one with my mother and sister," he heard himself say. He slid a sidelong glance, as if Hugh's reaction mattered. When the reporter raised his brows, prodding him to continue, Hector added, "I'd come home on weekends. Second year at college, full of myself. But I felt it was my duty to check up on Mom and Calista."

"Were your parents divorced?"

"Dad passed when Calista was just a toddler. I was in elementary school."

"So you were the man of the house."

"The big man, trying to be responsible. When I wasn't partying it up or sleeping with too many sorority girls."

"No harm, no foul. Lots of young men cut loose in college."

"Yeah, well, I woke up Saturday afternoon with a bitch of a hangover. Mom asked me to run to the grocery store—probably because she wanted to make a meal celebrating my return. I refused. Calista was in junior high, great kid, always laughing. She knew I'd never get my ass off the couch. She offered to do the shopping with Mom."

"They were hit on the way back?"

"Three houses down from where we lived." The dreadful memory pressed down in a flash of images. Paramedics running. The blood pooling beneath his kid sister. But he was determined to get through this and so he added, "Mom died instantly. Calista survived being thrown through the Buick's window. A miracle, really."

Hugh's expression was rife with sympathy. "From what I found on the Internet, she's doing great. Did you know Philadelphia Big Sisters just gave her a *second* award? And it looks like her accounting firm is one of the best in the city. She's amazing."

The compliment unspooled something inside Hector, a ball of pain bound up inside him for years. "Yeah, she's doing well. She has full range of motion from the waist up. Being in a wheelchair has never stopped her from leading a productive life. When she's not working or volunteering at Big Sisters, she has a passion for taking cruises with her women friends. She's the life of the party."

"She doesn't blame you."

"No."

Hugh took this in with an intense curiosity. "And

your ex-wives? How do they fit in?"

Having come this far was there any harm in finishing the story? Expelling a breath, Hector said, "After we buried Mom, Calista thought we both needed something. I'd dropped out of school, a year went by and another—eventually she talked me into joining a group at the community center for families in crisis. I met Sil there. She'd been driving to work when a drunk driver came down a highway entrance ramp."

"I can't imagine."

"You don't know Sil. She's a lot like Calista— indomitable. She's really generous in a way most people aren't. When we met, I was an emotional cripple with a black cloud around my head. She made me feel good just because she was in the room. Reason enough to marry her."

"You didn't love her?"

A tough question. At the time, he thought he did. "More than anything I wanted to help her walk again," he said, finding an odd relief in rehashing events he preferred not to think about. "One of those impossible wishes, but I was smart enough to know I'd help myself if I got her back on her feet. It took a lot of therapy, but she got there. It wasn't until after she dumped me and Bunny, my second wife, was in the process of dumping me, that I caught on to my real motivations."

"Which were?"

"I was trying to make amends for what happened to my sister."

"Honorable, if unrealistic."

"Yeah, I finally got that. Even did a stint in the military thinking good deeds erase bad. It didn't rid me of the guilt."

"You care about Calista, right? I'm sure she knows. Maybe it's enough."

Not even close, but he didn't counter the statement.

144

"She lost so much on my account. Never dated, never fell in love or even talked about having a family. Do you know what it's like to spend the best years of your life in a broken body? I don't. Hell, and I've tried to imagine it. I can't even wrap my brain around the idea. And here's my kid sister, the sweetest woman in the world, and she's stunning. Long, black hair and a sparkling personality— guys should be falling all over her. She rarely gets a second glance, and she wheels around our old neighborhood with something nice to say to everyone. Why isn't she bitter? How does she make an ugly situation so beautiful?"

"It's not ugly. You're describing someone who refuses to be a victim. Between the two of you, *you're* the one with the handicap."

"I'll buy that. I can't even imagine Calista acting like a victim. Hell, she has a temper like Medusa. I know not to arrive late if she's invited me for Sunday dinner." He dragged his hand across his scalp then added, "All I'm saying is she deserved better."

"Some people find the good in any situation." Hugh slapped him on the knee, startling him. "I think I'd like your sister. She's remarkable."

"She is." Hector's heart felt like lead but he couldn't resist adding, "I guess it would be easier if she hated me. She should. If the situation were reversed, I don't think I'd rise to her level. I'm not made of the same stuff."

"I think you are."

With deliberate care, Hugh closed his laptop. He seemed to process everything he'd been told, his attention moving aimlessly across the grass.

Men rarely shared their deepest wounds. Doing so had changed the air between them in a nearly tangible way. Friendships were forged on less than a conversation about a shattering past. If they were becoming friends, Hector was glad for it.

As if sensing the same, Hugh said, "I understand

145

why your sister can't blame you. You're a good guy. More importantly, you aren't responsible for the accident."

"Is that your way of apologizing for snooping around in my past?"

Hugh lifted his hands skyward. "It's the best I've got."

"I'll take it."

"Thanks." Hugh checked his watch. "I should go to The Second Chance, see if Birdie is with Finney. I hear Finney's taking the robbery hard."

The change of topics was a relief. "I'm nervous about what Wish has planned next," Hector said, wondering what she had in store. Odds were she was only getting started. She'd do something worse than rob Finney or hit up the stores on Liberty Square. "Now that Chief Burnes has a bead on Willet and James Pearson, what's to stop her from replacing them with new scum? She might fan out across Liberty, decide to break into a dozen residences. I hope the ritzy homes on North Street have burglar alarms."

"Hell, I hadn't thought of that."

"You should."

Hector was about to add something when instinct tickled his spine. An odd sensation followed, as if someone was watching him.

He wheeled his gaze across the center green's rolling lawn. Far from the bustle of people coming and going at the courthouse, beyond the maple trees where the kids were playing soccer, he caught movement. His attention landed on the sugar shack where locals brewed maple syrup in the late winter months.

Time scudded to a halt.

Beside the sugar shack, the last person he cared to see gave a hearty wave.

Chapter 10

She wore a shoulder length wig as sleek as mink and so deep sable in color, a hint of purple shone in each strand. Heavy eyeliner gave the illusion of almond-shaped eyes. Combined with the smoky grey sheath dripping from her shoulders in silky folds, she was nearly unrecognizable.

"Close your mouth, Birdie. You look like a fish out of water." Wish tipped a scented cheek. "Don't you have a kiss for your mother?"

Birdie's capacity for thought vanished.

The shock rendering her mute gave her mother a dangerous advantage. "What *are* you wearing? Is my little bitch slumming today?" She plucked at Birdie's tee shirt then rubbed her palms together as if dispelling a rank odor. "What happened to your pretty clothes? I was particularly fond of the leather jacket."

Still she couldn't respond. It was as if her mother's presence was toxin eating away at her defenses.

Undeterred, Wish threaded her fingers through her sable wig. "Isn't it great? My Asian look—men love it." She tossed her head, fluttering the strands around her cheeks. "Don't you love how it makes me look mysterious? Like a pearl of the Orient. I picked it up in Atlanta."

"You should go." The words spilled out of their own volition. Although she was grateful her voice had returned Birdie wasn't sure she could suppress the quicksand emotions urging her feet toward the door. "Just go. Nobody wants you here. This was a peaceful, sleepy town until you charged in."

"How can I leave? There's a bounty on my head. Haven't you heard?"

"You've been hacking into the newspaper's computers for weeks."

"I don't see how the events are related."

She did, of course. But she enjoyed poking at her daughter as if Birdie were a caged bear. It was an old game, the taunts, the ridicule, with her mother always having the upper hand.

"You hacked into the computers, so the bounty for your capture was posted on the Internet," Birdie said with as much calm as she could muster. For once she wouldn't cede power. She'd try to fight back. "You want to think your actions never bring repercussions but they do. You brought this on yourself."

"Bullshit. Anyone stupid enough to call out the hounds is asking for punishment."

"So you'll punish the town?" The limits to her mother's desire for revenge were hard to fathom. "How's this? I'll get the website taken down, make sure all the bounty hunters are fired. Not that there are many left— you've scared most of them away. I'll take care of it, if you promise to leave us alone."

"*Us?* Are you talking about the poor saps living in this wretched town? Birdie, you don't think you're one of them. Do you?" Wish stopped, her eyes growing dull as malice snuffed out all traces of human feeling. "I didn't come here just to punish those trying to capture me. We both know I can't be caught. If you're curious, I've come for something else."

"Tell me what it is." If it were within her power, she'd get it. Anything, to make her mother leave.

"It's not something you can steal."

"Maybe I can. I'll try." Shame coursed through her. She was no longer a thief. She was trying to become something else—something better. "I've given it up, but I'll do it one last time if you'll go."

"It's impossible. What I want can't be stolen."

The conversation's oblique turn was maddening. There was no prying out the truth if Wish chose to hide her real motives. Whatever it was she desired, she'd go to great lengths to win it. Not the rubies Birdie had inherited—she could ask for them outright. It didn't matter what Birdie had thought she'd say if the request were made, how she'd planned to refuse to give up gems that were rightfully hers. Rooted before her mother, she was helpless. She could no more stand up to Wish than learn to speak Japanese.

Birdie clenched and unclenched her fists. "This isn't your typical scam. You've already hurt people—children, even. Do you understand what you did to Snoops? She has a broken leg, and it could've been worse. You could've killed her."

Wish batted her eyes. "Oh, stop it. So I drove too close. Is it my fault the brat went off the road? She was bicycling at breakneck speed. She should've watched where she was going."

"She was watching *you,* tailing her."

"Not my problem."

"It *is* your problem if the police slap you into a jail cell for endangering a child. And what about Finney? Give back the money you stole." The need to help the cook made her thrust out her hand. "I'm serious, mother. Give it back."

"Don't tell me you care about a woman who flips burgers for a living."

"I care about Finney, and Snoops and everyone else here. They're my friends. Is the idea really beyond your

149

comprehension? I won't let you hurt them. I don't even understand *why* you want to hurt them. They aren't rich, and they aren't your usual targets."

All of which begged the question dogging her for days. What made Liberty a draw for a grifter? Los Angeles or New York City were preferred targets, or Miami with its multitude of wealthy retirees. Cities gave cover for a criminal looking to remain anonymous. In a town the size of Liberty, Wish increased the odds of capture. Each day she prolonged her stay, the stakes rose. What prize did the town offer for her to take the risk?

Birdie was still puzzling it out when her mother said, "What's Theodora like? I understand you've become close to our distant cousin." Wish stroked her neck with faint irritation, her lips pursed with a hint of disdain. "I never did understand the details of our lineage. Perhaps I can't get over the part about a family driven to ruin by war. From all accounts, we were terribly rich. However, it is fascinating how a black slave came all the way from South Carolina in the 1860s to settle here, of all places."

"Theodora's ancestor was a freedwoman, not a slave. Our ancestor Lucas freed her before she left South Carolina. He loved her."

"Details, details."

Birdie's patience was wearing thin. "It wouldn't hurt if you learned something about Justice Postell," she snapped. "She had real courage. Grit. Her descendants, including Theodora, helped make this town what it is today. Anyone can understand why Lucas adored her."

"You're such a romantic. Who cares about star-crossed lovers from the 1800s? I can't benefit from the dead. Now, Theodora is another matter. How *does* a woman her age reign over Liberty? A regular Queen Elizabeth. Or . . . what was the name of the actress in Monaco? The one who died?"

"Princess Grace," Birdie supplied, desperate for the

conversation to end. "What does she have to do with Theodora?"

The query flashed annoyance across Wish's face. "Don't be obtuse," she said. There was something feral in her eyes, a savagery brought forth by the mention of Theodora. "Our cousin is admired by so many. It's not a stretch to say people love Theodora. *She* interests me."

The need to protect Theodora unblocked the fear imprisoning Birdie's heart. "Stay away from her," she said, advancing. "She's been good to me, really good, and I won't let you hurt her. If you go anywhere near her, I'll—"

The threat died in midair. What, what would she do? She couldn't back the threat, couldn't even find the strength to pull her cell from her purse and dial 911 to bring the police. The abuse she'd endured as a child, the sweet compliments followed by unexpected beatings, the months of dining in fine restaurants playing the role of sweet baby that inevitably led to abandonment in trailer parks with the man she'd thought was her father, or with other, lost souls who owed Wish money or favors—the past had stunted every natural defense.

Laughter thick with mockery bubbled from her mother. "Has my little bitch lost her voice again?" she asked, stabbing at Birdie's paltry self-confidence. "Such a pity. I rather enjoy your fiery streak. It's quite like mine. Isn't rage delicious, the freedom it lends to lash out? My favorite emotion. Nothing else comes close."

"You're despicable."

Her mother's expression became predatory like a shark scenting blood. "I'm curious," she said, changing tack. "What did Theodora think of *my* clue?"

"What clue?"

"My text message."

"You sent her a text?" It was a horribly intimate form of harassment.

"You know how it goes—one of those spur-of-the-moment inspirations you can't resist. And why not? Wasn't I the one who sent you to Liberty last summer to follow the clue handed down in our family? It seemed time to invent one myself—a new clue leading to a new treasure. Naturally I sent it to your dear friend Theodora."

"What did it say?" Birdie wheeled between fear and anger. Why hadn't Theodora mentioned it? Any direct contact put her in danger. "Stop playing around and tell me."

"My, you're touchy."

"Tell me!"

"Oh, all right." Wish paused for effect. *"Earn your Liberty if you dare."*

The meaning seemed pathetically obvious. "You're wasting your time," Birdie said, willing a modicum of calm into her voice. "She won't fall for blackmail. She knows it will keep her on the hook for years. She's not stupid."

"Try again, daughter. You're not even close."

"Then explain. I'm tired of this game."

"It means," Wish said slowly, "I'll injure her in ways you can't imagine if she doesn't give me what I want. Be careful, Birdie. There's a firestorm coming. You can't stop it."

The chance to form a rebuttal disappeared. The honed senses that kept Wish from capture sharpened her expression. She whirled around. Birdie did the same, following her line of sight.

In the nave's aisle stood a plain-faced woman not unlike the one Birdie had conjured in her daydream. Her apron was dusted with flour. The rolling pin in her grip wobbled. But her eyes were flinty.

"I've called the police," she said.

Wish fled the church.

Theodora had reached her trusty Cadillac when

Chief Burnes charged out of the station waving his arms like a man attempting flight.

"She's been sighted," he shouted. He jogged over to her car. "The pastor's wife called it in, down on Grant Street."

"Olivia Martin?" Olivia baked the best apple strudel in the county, but she always found the corner in a crowded room. Loud noises made her jump. Needless to say, she was no match for Wish. "She didn't wrangle with the devil, did she? Olivia's so bashful she'd run from a testy child."

"Not her," the chief said. He laid a careful palm on Theodora's back. "Wish was arguing with Birdie."

The president of Philadelphia's Mecca Freight and other, less respectable enterprises in The City of Brotherly Love surveyed the center green like an emperor pleased with his domain.

"Nice town," Nick said when Hector, stunned by his appearance, reached the park bench beside the sugar shack. "Reminds me of a TV show from a long time ago. Hit show was on the air before you were born. It was real popular."

His uncle meant *The Andy Griffith Show,* not that a chat about 1960s TV was necessary. "Why the hell are you in Liberty?" Hector demanded.

"Thought I'd stop by." When Hector glowered, Nick added, "I have business in Akron, plus I'm tired of calls from your fiancé, Charlene. The chick needs something. Valium would be a good place to start."

"Ex-fiancé."

"You sure?" Nick repositioned his massive body on the bench, his fleshy thighs spreading out and his man-breasts nearly bursting from his starched white shirt. "A woman gets that fired up she's still got you in her system.

Screaming in my ear, begging me to do something so she'll get her money back—I've had enough. Spider's taking her calls now. Not happy about it, either."

His uncle glanced toward the sugar shack and Hector's spirits reached an all-time low. The day had already provided enough pathos after the discussion with Hugh, who'd thankfully wandered off to The Second Chance Grill in search of Birdie. Now Hector had . . . *this* to deal with.

Like anyone with smarts in his head, he knew to steer clear of his uncle's second-in-command, Spider. The beast sprouted sweat on everyone he passed. Muscles wrapped his six-foot frame and he really did have a black widow spider stamped on his mouth. The nasty bug sprawled legs down Spider's chin and up to his nostrils. No one knew why he got the tattoo back in his shady youth. The guy looked like a fearsome brick wall complete with graffiti.

Thankfully Spider was staying in the shadows. Hector scanned the center green. Total calm, and he was sure no one had spotted the beast.

"What's he doing here?" He pivoted in a circle to double-check that the kids playing soccer weren't scared senseless. But the gods were smiling; the kids didn't notice the monster lurking in the shadows.

"Relax. Where I go, Spider goes," Nick said peevishly. "Since when did you get stupid?"

"What do you want?"

"Watch your tone. I'm the one who'll do the asking." Nick yanked on his red silk tie, loosening it. "You been to see your cousins in Cleveland? Or your Great Aunt Rena in Youngstown? She'll put a lamb on a spit, fix you up real nice."

"I don't have time to see family."

"You've come all the way to Ohio. Don't be a stranger."

"Uncle Nick, I'm not in Ohio to socialize. I'm working."

"Yeah? I didn't get the details from your crazy fiancé. 'Course it's hard to get information when a woman's on a rant."

Hector's composure started to slip, but he hung on. Offer a simple explanation and his uncle would leave. Given the choice, he preferred *not* to introduce the family mobster to anyone in Liberty. It was embarrassing enough to run into Uncle Nick at the occasional wedding or funeral.

"I'm here on a job," he said. "There's a bounty for a female criminal. I'm trying to catch her."

"You're here chasing some dame? Big leap from your last job playing around in the stock market."

"It's temporary work. Once she's caught, I'll find something else."

"Let me guess. Next you'll say you're joining the police academy. You switch jobs faster than women change hairstyles."

"Actually, I'm thinking about something in sales or marketing."

"You mean something on the up-and-up," his uncle said with distaste. "You're just like your father, may he rest in peace. Too busy toeing the line to take care of yourself."

"If he were alive he'd say you've sunk so low, you don't know you're standing in shit."

Never before had he spoken so boldly to his uncle, but he was still raw from the conversation with Hugh. Plus he'd had his ass whipped this morning in Bongo's parking lot. He would've fared worse if his elderly companion didn't pack a Winchester and the nerves to use it. The image he had of himself—successful, confident, a can-do guy—wasn't faring well today. All things considered, he'd rather be in Philly dreaming up a do-over and scouring Monster.com for work.

Spider leapt from the shadows to slap him on the

side of the head. "Watch how you talk to the boss man," he said, a spray of spittle accompanying the warning.

"Touch me again and you'll pick your teeth off the floor." A lousy threat he couldn't back. Landing a punch on someone as dangerous as Spider wasn't smart, even if it was tempting.

"Oh, yeah? Try it."

His uncle raised a subduing hand. "Spider, wait in the car. Let me talk to my nephew."

"You sure, boss?"

"Get moving."

The sulky giant left.

Hector dreaded asking, but couldn't resist. "Why did you stop by? Guilt-tripping me about visiting relatives isn't the best use of your time."

Uncle Nick rubbed his thumb across the thick gold of his Rolex, his expression filling with mirth and deadly calculation. "You really don't know? I'm here because it's time."

"Time for what?"

Deftly Nick sidestepped the question. "That crazy fiancé of yours—how much do you owe her? And what about your ex-wives? Bad thing for a man to hurt the women he loves. I could do without the crazy bitch, but Sil and Bunny are real nice."

"I'll pay them back. Every cent."

"What? By chasing some dame for the cash prize?" Nick asked with thick impatience. "Who you looking for anyway? Some chick knocking off banks? A modern day Bonnie without her Clyde?"

"I'd rather not go into it."

"Fine by me. I don't really care. All I'm saying is you waste your time on the wrong jobs. Why not go into a more lucrative career? This nine-to-five shit don't pay off. Know what I mean?"

"Where are you going with this, Uncle Nick?"

"Work for me. You won't believe how good you have it. For incentive, I'll pay back every cent you owe your women. Call it a signing bonus."

"I can't."

"Says who? You're family. I'll take good care of you. Haven't I been good to your cousin Freddie?"

"Sure, if we aren't counting the murder rap."

"Attempted murder, and he got off." Nick's eyes blazed. "The prosecutor couldn't make anything stick."

He couldn't, an immaterial point. What *did* matter? Most of the Levendakis tribe led honest, productive lives. They stayed the hell away from Nick's underworld machinations and the temptations of reaping an ill-gotten fortune. Maybe Freddie had gone the wrong way. But Hector was like most of his relatives even if he'd failed at a dozen jobs, including the latest stint as a day-trader that had resulted in the loss of all his savings—and much of his ex-wives' and ex-fiancé's savings too.

"What do you say?" Nick asked. "Why not give up this wild goose chase, come back home and work for me?"

A queasy disgust rolled through Hector. "I'm not cut out for it," he said.

"You'll adapt. What else can you do? You're too old to learn a trade, and all your fancy schooling hasn't done you no good. I've never seen a man screw up so many jobs. It's your special talent." Nick let the brutal facts sink in before adding, "Son, this here is the end of the road. I'm all you've got."

Chapter 11

"Theodora, *why* didn't you tell me about the text from my mother? This is exactly what I've been afraid of, Wish going after you because we're close. She hates the idea of me having a real relationship with anyone. It goes against, I don't know, her twisted code of ethics. And you're family even if I didn't know about you until last year. I'm sure she hates that most of all, how you've given me something worth having—a real family. Why didn't you say *something?*"

The tirade wasn't constructive. With effort, Birdie reeled in her temper.

They'd paused beneath an oak tree so tall the branches cradled the heavens. The view was magnificent, an undulating sweep of field and forest stretching for miles at the southern end of Theodora's property. The horizon was laced with a thousand leaves, the fresh green of spring as the trees unfurled a new year's glory.

"Are you done railing at me? I've said I'm sorry." Theodora kicked the mud from her hiking boots. "Blast it all—what did Wish say to you in the church?"

"She said there's a firestorm coming."

"Poppycock."

"You think? It sounded like she wanted to hurt you. After what she's done to Snoops and Finney, you should take this seriously. Is it any wonder I'm upset?"

"You're making a mountain out of a molehill. If the fool comes near, I'll send her to kingdom come. I swear, I will."

"Dreaming about taking a pot shot doesn't mean you will. And I wouldn't want you to."

Theodora chewed this around. "I could make an exception," she said. "Just this once."

"Talk, talk, talk." Birdie leaned against the oak's sturdy trunk. "Will you explain *why* you told everyone but me about the message?"

Was an explanation necessary?

Birdie knew why everyone was handling her like crystal. They were concerned she'd shatter if she had another run-in with her mother. True, the confrontation in the church had rattled her more than she wished to admit. It didn't mean she would be kept out of the loop, especially if Wish was threatening Theodora.

"C'mon, now," Theodora called from over her shoulder. Her pace quickened. "We both need the fresh air. Clear our heads."

Following, Birdie said, "I'm waiting. Why didn't you say anything?"

"Lordy, why would I? You think I don't understand what Wish has done to you? She taught you how to work in her scams when you were just a wee thing. She hurt and abused you, and left you living on your own when you were a teenager. She's done all that but she's never mothered you."

"At least you have." Much of Theodora's advice was like a blunt instrument right over the head, but she meant well. She cared.

The statement put a watery smile on Theodora's lips. "I've tried to mother you. Mind you, it hasn't been easy," she admitted. "You're as stubborn as they come and more apt to race into a wall than listen to good advice. I've seen mules with more potential than you, and they tend to be nasty creatures."

"Think it's genetic? The stubbornness? You're the same way."

"Like hell I am. I'm sensible to a fault. You might say I'm a regular Dalai Lama." Having issued the preposterous statement, Theodora picked up the pace, her tiny frame attacking the rough terrain like a woman half her age. When Birdie caught up, she added, "I am sorry. I should've told you about the text message. *Earn your liberty if you dare.* Cain and Jezebel, I can't get a fix on what it means."

"Don't drive yourself crazy trying to figure it out. If I had to guess, it means 'pay up or I'll cause more trouble.' Another one of my mother's famous threats."

"I'm not paying a ransom. I already hashed it out with Finney and Ethel Lynn. We agreed it wouldn't work. Your mother will just come back later to cause more trouble. I'll be leaking cash for the rest of my days."

"When did you discuss this with Finney and Ethel Lynn?"

Theodora heaved out a sigh. "They've been staying at my house, a couple of regular freeloaders. Finney's back home with her kids—understandable since she's been robbed—but Ethel Lynn? She shows up every night. I can't get rid of her."

The two women battled like gladiators. How they spent the night together and avoided bloodshed was anyone's guess.

"How long has this been going on?" Birdie asked.

"Oh, a few days now. They got it in their heads I need protection."

"Should Hector or Hugh spend the night?" If anything happened, it was better to have a man on the premises. "We don't know who my mother hired. What if

161

CHAPTER 11

she sends someone to your house?"

"To do what? Scare me?" Theodora stopped to catch her breath. "I'm not scared of Wish Kaminsky or the lowlifes she travels with. Didn't I take one of them down this morning at Bongo's? I'm more worried about keeping you protected. Your mother's as sneaky as Mata Hari."

It was probably true. "How about this? Hector stays with you. I've got Hugh for protection."

"I'll think about it."

There was no sense insisting. Nagging Theodora wouldn't change her mind. If she refused to let Hector spend the night, there were other alternatives. Birdie made a mental note to call Chief Burnes later. He'd have a patrol car to swing by throughout the night without informing his headstrong friend.

Changing track, she said, "I'm glad you won't let my mother put the town up for ransom." She neglected to add that she'd personally been willing to do whatever her mother asked to persuade her to leave. A momentary weakness. "She'd take your money then come back for more. Scary, if you think about it."

"We're quite the pair, aren't we? A mean old woman and a girl so afraid of her shadow, she can't make good choices."

"You aren't mean, and I *have* been making good choices." Great choices—hadn't she given up life as a pickpocket? True, she'd nearly thrown away her ethics in a misdirected offer to rid Liberty of her mother, and she still felt ashamed. But she hadn't. "Wasn't it smart to open the *Liberty Post* with Hugh? The county needed a good daily newspaper. And I'm settled now. I own real estate."

"I'm not talking about a mortgage," Theodora snapped. "You dilly-dally when you ought to make the one good choice sure to plant your feet on the ground. Why delay?"

She meant Hugh and the speed bumps they'd

162

encountered during their engagement. "He tried to patch things up," Birdie admitted, wondering why she kept throwing roadblocks in his path. Reflecting on how poorly she'd treated him, she added, "I've been keeping him in the dog house. Not the smartest move. I feel bad about it."

"You should. I'm ashamed of you."

"I'm ashamed of me too. Sometimes when we disagree I put a wall around my emotions when I ought to try to find a compromise. It's stupid and it's childish."

"Then stop doing it." Theodora thwacked her on the arm. "Sometimes you don't have the sense God gave a billy goat. What's wrong with you, Birdie? Don't you love him?"

"More than anything. More than—" The emotion flooding through her sent the explanation fleeing from her head. Hugh made her feel whole and protected and alive. Maybe he'd moved out in a fit of frustration, but he deserved her forgiveness. He deserved more, deserved everything she had to offer. Still, she couldn't help but add, "I'm not sure I'm cut out for marriage. What if I screw it up? I don't have a great track record with relationships."

"Hells bells, you don't have any track record. Before Hugh, you wandered the earth stealing from others and making yourself miserable. He loves you, child—loves you heart and soul. He never would've moved out if you'd given him reason to stay. Did you?"

"Not really," she said with remorse. "I didn't understand how much I love him until he'd gone. Stupid, isn't it? I should've understood how much he means to me."

"There's time a'plenty to mend your relationship. Why not get started? This nonsense with your mother barreling into town causing all sorts of ruckus, it'll pass. In the meantime, don't lose sight of the one person who loves you more than I do. And Lord knows I care about you."

With surprising tenderness, she drew Birdie close. Displays of affection were rare for Theodora, and Birdie knew to savor the long, rocking hug. If she'd waited

163

decades for maternal love, for the wisdom and guidance she'd never before known, did it matter? Theodora was now a permanent fixture in her life, a nurturing presence and a guiding light. Birdie's love for her had never been stronger.

Nor had her love for Hugh.

When they drew apart, she said, "I should call Hugh. He's probably looking for me."

"I'm sure he is."

Birdie reached into her purse . . . and discovered her cell phone missing.

With ill-repressed glee, Wish scrolled through the email on her daughter's phone. One note in particular caught her interest, an invitation to a birthday party. Her mind spun a glorious web as she reread the mail sent by Ethel Lynn Percible. The hyperactive grand dame was probably as rich as Theodora, her residence loaded with jewelry and cash. Easy pickings.

Or was it time to go further than simple burglary? Wish eagerly chased after her thoughts.

Why simply rob Ethel Lynn? There were countless ways to inflict additional damage. Snatch the best goods tucked away in the house and destroy the rest? Take a hammer to her priceless antiques? Striking at another person her daughter cared about was as invigorating as a day at the race track.

James Pearson coughed, evidently to get her attention. When she met his gaze coldly, he sauntered up. With his kid brother stewing in the Liberty jail, he was in the dumps. Moody, irritable—she wished he'd snap out of it. She needed him sharp for tomorrow's ploy in Liberty Square.

"The last man is here," he announced. "Ready to talk to them?"

"More than ready."

Wrap up the meeting, and she could leave this rat hole thirty minutes outside Liberty. The dilapidated warehouse reeked of something nasty, a byproduct from its former life as a manufacturing facility. Whatever it was, ammonia or worse, it wasn't good for her skin. She made a mental note to schedule a week at the spa after she finished tearing down Liberty.

She remembered James, shuffling his feet like a truculent child. "How many did you hire?" she asked.

"I got twenty-four guys."

"That's all?"

He lifted his bony shoulders to his ears. "You said no druggies. I didn't have time to find anyone else, and you said no one local."

"No one from Liberty, that's correct."

"They're all from Willoughby, about thirty minutes from here. All clean—not one drug user in the bunch, just like you said."

"I can't risk using drug addicts." They wouldn't follow orders. The men needed to work fast and with precision. "We're fine with twenty-four. Twenty-five, if your brother is released in the morning."

In the doorway to the main warehouse, James halted. "What if Willet doesn't get out? Will you get him a lawyer?"

"I'll think about it."

"Bullshit. Will you or not?"

His defiance had her gritting her teeth. "We're partners, aren't we? If he isn't out tomorrow, I'll have him lawyered up in a jiffy. I know a great firm in Akron. I'll give them a call."

She'd do nothing of the sort, but it was best to give the dullard hope. Use him, lose him—once she got what she'd come for, she'd dump Beavis and his stupid brother on the side of the road. Preferably on a road in a southern state on her way to greener pastures.

Concentrating on the task at hand, she appraised the men assembled in the center of the dingy warehouse. They were all young like James and probably just as dimwitted, two-bit criminals hungry for an easy score. They'd do. If everything went according to plan, she'd put Finney's six thousand and change to good use.

Wish held up the cook's money. The wad of cash was a temptation luring the men forward. "You want it?" she asked. "It's yours—tomorrow—if you do exactly what I say."

In the living room's dusky light, Hugh sent a smile rife with compassion. "Don't take it too hard," he said. "Wish stealing your phone isn't my idea of a disaster. She's capable of so much worse. You're fine. Nothing else matters."

Joining him on the couch, Birdie kicked off her shoes and drew her feet onto the coffee table beside his. A nourishing quiet surrounded them, as if the danger posed by her mother had abolished the bickering and hurt feelings plaguing their relationship.

Times of crisis had a way of putting everything in perspective, of revealing bonds that were solid. Their personal issues were inconsequential in light of the harm befalling the citizens of Liberty, the thefts and injuries of people they cared about, the mindless acts of cruelty brought about by Wish's hand.

In the hours since the confrontation with her mother at the church, Birdie had been gratefully delivered first to Theodora then Hugh, the transfer carried out in a whispered phone call after the long walk in the woods.

Brewing tea in Theodora's kitchen, she pretended not to overhear the hurried words and shared concern of the two people who loved her most. It had been a relief to learn Hugh would cut short an interview to ensure he arrived home first. Those spare minutes were used to tidy up the living room and refresh the coffee table with a vase of spring daisies. For a man driven to critique any detail beneath his exacting standards, he was endowed with a softer side.

The flowers, with their message of hope and renewal, drew her appreciative gaze. "I guess I should be happy my mother only took my cell," she said at last. "It's dumb luck she didn't take my wallet. Not sure why she didn't. Three hundred inside."

"Learn how to use checking and you won't have to carry much cash."

"Hugh—"

"Got it. I'm backing off." But he didn't, at least not in the way that mattered. Tentatively he pressed his palm to her thigh. In tacit approval she leaned her shoulder into his, and he began making slow circles across her jeans, his caress more soothing than sexual. "You're a cash-only girl. Not that life without a debit card strikes me as appealing. I couldn't live without one, but a checking account isn't your thing. Never was, never will be."

"I don't know about never, but I do need a refresher course in basic accounting."

"Let me know when you're ready."

"Deal." She regarded his fingers, moving gently and spiraling warmth through her rib cage. Unable to resist, she inched closer. "How did we do today?"

"The newspaper?" He returned his hand to his lap. It seemed a great loss. "For most of the afternoon we were cutting it close. Snoops ran an install, which slowed us down. Every computer in the place was on the fritz for about twenty minutes. Something to do with art files."

"Did you transmit to the printer in time?"

"By the skin of our teeth. It would've been easier if you'd been around. The new hires did their bit, but they don't write copy with your finesse. The skinny girl, Betsy? She has a nice style but nothing close to yours. Plus she gets weepy."

"Weepy?"

"She's wrapped tighter than tape. Snoops was downing cookies and trying to fix the install, and Betsy was sobbing at her desk. She snapped right out of it as soon as her copy reappeared on the screen. Until it did, she had the rest of us thinking about cowering under our desks. She's worth the drama, though. Best writer on the staff if we're not counting you."

"Or *you.*"

"I don't count. My thing's investigative journalism. Without your human interest stories, our readership wouldn't grow so fast."

It wasn't the first time he'd complimented her natural copywriting abilities. Hugh nagged about the small stuff, like her habits of dropping clothes on the floor or leaving dishes in the sink, but he also tried to burnish her self-esteem with praise. In future, why not make an effort to appreciate the compliments and turn a deaf ear to the criticism? There was no changing a bone-deep personality trait, and Hugh *was* a perfectionist. With himself, and everyone else. Accepting the sharper side of his temperament would smooth the rough patches in their relationship.

"I like writing copy, turning a jumble of words into something useful, maybe even compelling," she said. She liked his touch more, and glanced hungrily at his hands. "Are you staying the night? I checked your calendar—no appointments."

"You bet." Satisfaction rimmed his mouth. Just as quickly, he grew thoughtful. "Birdie, I don't mind sleeping on the couch. Seeing your mother took a lot out of you, and I don't want to take advantage. Hit the sack early. You don't look good. Frankly, I've never seen you this tired."

There was no disputing the assessment. The last days had sapped her strength. Her throat was scratchy and her stomach was still roiling after the run-in at the church. Add in an unexpected stroll across the acres behind Theodora's house, and she'd gladly sleep through tomorrow, skip the entire day in hopes her mother would disappear before she awoke.

Yet she yearned for a night clinging to Hugh. Snuggling to his solid form as she slumbered would sustain her through whatever crisis tomorrow might bring.

Boldly, she took his hand and settled it back on her thigh. "Why don't we share the bed?" Despite her exhaustion, she sent a flirty look. "I promise to behave myself."

The suggestive comment put a predatory gleam in his eyes. "Don't tempt me. I'd like nothing more than to make love to you." He swallowed, sending his Adam's Apple bobbing in his throat. "This is more of a dry spell than I'd like. It's been tough."

"Then come to bed with me."

"Tomorrow, after you're rested. Tonight I'm on the couch."

Laughter bubbled up inside her, but his expression warned her off. "You act like you need to stay close to the front door in case—" She stopped and put it all together. "Do you think someone will break in tonight?"

"After what happened to Finney, I'm not taking any chances. Hector thinks we should be prepared for anything."

"Where is he?"

"In his RV."

"He's out in our parking lot?" He'd left his home on wheels beside the barn. The last she'd heard, he was picking up a rental car. "Why doesn't he come inside?"

"From the looks of it, he's stewing. I'd take the blame, but I think it's something else."

169

Guilt flashed through Hugh's devil dark gaze, and she held him at arm's length. "What did you do to upset him?" she asked. He'd been giving Hector a hard time from the moment he arrived in Liberty. It needed to stop.

He gave a brief explanation about fishing around in Hector's past then added, "I felt like shit after we talked. I really shouldn't have pried."

"What did you find?"

"I can't go into it. Doing so feels like I'm breaking a confidence. If you're interested, ask Hector to tell you about it," Hugh said, trailing his fingers across her neck. He seemed torn between an oddly protective impulse toward Hector and a desire to ravish her. If he let her vote, she'd choose door number two.

Trying vainly to resist the allure of his touch, she said, "I hope you didn't hurt his feelings. I think he's one of the loneliest people I've ever met. He tries to hide it, but it's obvious. Once we're through this mess with my mother, we should fix him up with someone."

"What? Like a matchmaking service?" Hugh nipped at her ear. "We could have some fun, set him up with a woman who's impossible. Meade comes to mind. She's got 'handful' written all over her."

Birdie's half-sister *did* have a demanding personality. Driven, successful and drop-dead gorgeous, she wasn't presently dating. "They'd never get along. Hector is too lively and Meade's dignified. I can't visualize them together. Oil and water. They'd never mix."

"Meade wasn't too dignified to chase Anthony Perini around the block. Remember? Before he settled down with Mary?"

The story was familiar. "We didn't live here at the time," she reminded him. "Meade chasing Anthony sounds like overblown gossip, and I'm not asking her for the truth." She wound her arms around Hugh's waste. "What about Delia? She's quite a bit younger than Hector but she's bubbly. I think she's more his speed."

"He sure could use something to cheer him up." Hugh grew quiet. At last he added, "This afternoon, after I went to The Second Chance looking for you, I spotted him talking to an older man in the center green. More like arguing with him. The man didn't look familiar. I've got a hunch whatever they discussed got Hector down in the dumps."

"Why don't you talk to him? Hugh, he's a sweet man. You should stop baiting him."

"I'm done giving him a hard time. Feeling bad about it too, now that I know more about his background. He's a good guy." Hugh glanced at her, his eyes hooded. "As long as he stops flirting with you."

"He's harmless, trust me."

"No guy's harmless if he puts the moves on my woman. But if it makes you feel better, I'll talk to him . . . in a minute."

With a playfulness missing from their relationship for too long, he dragged her against his chest and brushed her mouth with the tempting hint of a kiss. Heat spun through her limbs. Then he sealed his mouth to hers with an affection shattering in intensity. Gentle, rough, titillating, sweet—he kissed her into a state of breathlessness.

Without warning, he set her away and struggled to his feet.

She wondered at his pained expression, the flush across his cheeks and the need flashing in his eyes. There was no question he wanted her, and she stared in confusion. On a muttered oath, he pivoted toward the kitchen.

Abandoned, she gaped at his retreating back. "Where are you going? We were just getting started."

"No, we're not. You need to eat then get some shut-eye."

She heard him rummaging around the kitchen, opening drawers and cupboards. The sign-song chime of the microwave, followed by the heavenly scent of chicken soup, urged her from the couch.

She stretched languidly, the remnants of his kiss still simmering in her blood. "You had time to cook?" she called.

"Takeout," came the crisp reply.

"I wish you'd take me. To the bedroom, to be specific."

A string of oaths, and the microwave banged shut. "You're killing me, Birdie," he shouted. "I'm trying to show how much I love you. If you need more proof, tomorrow I'll make pot roast and potatoes. I'll do it, if you promise to scrub the pots."

Pot roast and mashed potatoes—one of her favorite meals. "Sounds great."

"Soup's getting cold. Are you coming or not?"

On a smile, she followed him in.

Chapter 12

With Birdie safely tucked in bed, Hugh went to check on Hector.

Night was falling with a growing hush, the fields turning ashen and the last songbirds finding refuge for the night. At the side of the lot, the RV's red curtains were drawn to block out the world. Add in the whining notes of the country music drifting through the air, and it was a safe bet that Hector wasn't in the best mood.

Determined to get to the bottom of it, Hugh rapped on the door. "Anyone home?" No answer, and he rapped harder. "Open up. It's me."

"All right, already. Come in."

He did, and immediately his opinion of Hector inched up a few notches. The place was as neatly ordered and luxurious as a suite at a good hotel.

The RV's long, rectangular living room was surprisingly airy with a man-sized couch of buttery leather, built-in TV and golden oak storage cabinets. The kitchen, running along the opposite wall, boasted all the culinary delights—mixer, food processor, coffee grinder, even a crock pot for those busy days when there wasn't time to fool around in the kitchen hatching an inspired meal. The scents of sweet onion and sun-kissed tomato wafting from the stove beckoned Hugh forward.

"You can cook?" he asked, appraising Hector, splayed across the couch like the victim of a hit-and-run. A shiner was blackening beneath his left eye.

"What's the big deal? You think guys can't cook?" The moody oaf waved carelessly at the pot. "Give the soup a stir, will you?"

He did then he returned the man-sized utensil to the spoon rest. "How's the eye?" he asked. It looked painful.

"I've had worse. What's it to you?"

"Hey, I'm just asking." Unable to resist, Hugh grabbed a teaspoon from the drawer and sampled the rich broth. "This is really good."

"Fassolada. Greek bean soup. One of my mother's specialties, God rest her soul."

"I didn't have you pegged as a guy who knows his way around a kitchen." Not to mention the cabinets looked recently polished. Hugh sniffed, picking up a hint of lemon. "I sure didn't have you pegged as domestic."

Hector dragged himself into a sitting position. "It doesn't make me a girl. I like order, okay? Neat surroundings, something nice cooking on the stove—make a wisecrack about my feminine side, and I'll bloody your nose."

"Did you mop? The floor's shiny."

"I don't have a gym pass in this two-bit town. I needed to blow off steam."

"This is unnerving. It's like you're my twin." Faintly amused by the prospect, Hugh added, "I meant no offense. I get where you're coming from—I also like to cook. Always have." He left out the part about channeling his Zen while folding laundry in case it made *him* seem a touch too feminine.

"You cook?" Hector asked. "Talk about a shocker. I figured you were one of those pigs that trails chips across

174

the floor and pisses in the sink."

"Not even close."

"Favorite recipe?"

"Too many to name. I make a Prime Rib that brings down the house and the best Veal Marsala you've ever tasted."

"You're Italian?"

"No, but I love the cuisine. Anything with garlic and tomato gets my vote." With misgiving, he regarded the pistol lying on the table. "You seem down. You aren't planning to do anything stupid, are you?"

Hector looked at him like he'd grown a tail. "With the Glock? I was cleaning it." He stashed the gun in a hidden compartment beneath the couch's center cushion. When he'd finished, he cast a wary glance. "That's why you're here? To save me from myself? Pal, I'm not the type for theatrics."

"Good to know."

"I'm on top of the world."

Nowhere close, but there was no gain in pointing out the obvious. "After we talked this afternoon, you were arguing with a man in the center green. You seemed pretty upset."

"After we *talked?* You mean after you were nosing around in my past. What is it with reporters? You should stick to current events." He got up, checked the pot. After he'd wiped three dots of spatter from the counter and stirred once again, he appeared to rein in his temper. "Want some? I was getting ready to eat."

Hugh murmured his thanks, and two steaming bowls were deposited on the table. He gratefully dug in. Splitting the chicken soup with Birdie hadn't worked out as planned. She'd eaten like a jackal, finishing the takeout in record time before slipping off to bed.

Surreptitiously, he peered out the RV's window at the barn's second floor. He hoped she was sleeping soundly, spared from nightmares.

Following his gaze, Hector said, "Ease up. She's fine. No one can get close to the place without us seeing it."

A reassuring observation. If a car came into the lot, they'd have a bead on it before anyone got out.

Hugh sent a silent prayer heavenward that Wish and her accomplices would leave his beloved alone tonight. The tension was wearing Birdie out. All those second guesses about what would happen next and the further harm sure to befall the town—it kept her on a heightened state of alert sure to damage her health. The confrontation at the church only made matters worse. And he didn't know how to protect her. He was a reporter not a goddamn mystic. Knowing where Wish would strike next, or how, was beyond him.

Nudging him from his thoughts, Hector said, "I tried to talk to Theodora, convince her to let me stay at her place. It seemed like a good idea since you're here with Birdie."

"Theodora turned down the offer?"

"She said she's already cursed with an affliction she'd like to send straight to hell. No idea what she meant. Thirty seconds of angry old woman, and I knew to hang up."

"She means Ethel Lynn."

"She's spending the night with Theodora? I got the impression they didn't get along."

"Think guerilla warfare and enemy combatants. A cease-fire isn't possible. They've been at war for decades."

"About what?"

"A million perceived injustices. Both families have deep roots in Liberty. The Hatfields and the McCoys have nothing on the Percible-Hendricks feud. Add in unrequited love and more battles over land and treasure than you can imagine, and you get one fine mess." Hugh warmed to his story. "When she was young, Ethel Lynn was quite the catch. And a party animal, if you can believe it."

Hector regarded him doubtfully. "The old flirt was a catch? You sure?" He spooned soup around his bowl, considering. "Okay. I take it back. Peel three decades off her skin, and she was probably gorgeous."

"She was. I've seen the photos."

"How does the feud factor in?"

"Some of the bad blood has to do with The Second Chance Grill. It was started by Theodora's ancestor."

"Justice Postell, the freedwoman," Hector supplied. "Wait a second. I thought some doctor owned the restaurant now. Mary Chance, right?"

"That's right. She inherited it from her aunt. Another long story, but not as interesting as *how* her aunt came to own the restaurant in the first place. Which brings me back to Ethel Lynn during her wild youth."

Hector pushed his bowl away, clearly enjoying the story. "This is gonna be good."

"Yeah? It isn't, if you ask Ethel Lynn. She's been facing down Theodora's fury ever since. During one of the boozier phases of her youth, Ethel Lynn put together a poker game. She was always hosting parties, serving too much liquor and getting people in trouble. Theodora's husband showed up early. He was one of those people who never turned down free booze. A bunch of other people also came early, including Meg—Mary's aunt, the one who gave her the restaurant."

"Oh, man. Don't tell me. . ?"

"You got it. Theodora's husband was drunk, losing every hand. He'd taken over the restaurant after he married Theodora and totally mismanaged the place. Thought it was a losing proposition. So he put it up as a wager. Meg had four queens—and, by midnight, the deed to the restaurant."

"Man, that's bad." Hector looked up. "Hold on. If two ladies hate each other, why spend the night together?"

"You don't understand this town. There's hate, the feud . . . but the people have integrity. Pride. And beneath it all, love. If you ask me, Ethel Lynn and Theodora are the closest of friends. All that fire in the gut keeps the relationship interesting." The conversation had loosened Hector up, lending an opening. Treading carefully, Hugh switched topics. "Who was the man? The one you were arguing with in Liberty Square?"

The query bowed Hector's shoulders. "My Uncle Nick. He was in the area, thought he'd look me up."

"The uncle who's a—" Hugh sputtered to an embarrassed silence. He couldn't say *mobster* or *underworld character* without risking insult.

The meaning telegraphed instantly. "Yeah, *that* uncle," Hector said. "Basically he wants me to join the dark side. He probably thinks he's doing me a favor. I've tried a dozen jobs and failed at every one. I'm a loser."

"You've helped us hunt for Wish. That qualifies as a success."

"Not even close. She's still on the loose."

"True, but you nabbed Willet Pearson. Now the PD has a bead on one of her accomplices. It's a start. A good start, if you ask me."

"Hardly counts."

Providing a 'chin up' speech wasn't Hugh's strong suit. In truth he didn't have solid advice. He'd never drifted through life as Birdie had, or bounced from job to job like Hector. Understanding what he wanted in a career and the steps needed to achieve the dream had always been easy. It dawned that Birdie and Hector were common in some respects, how they waited for life to reveal the right path. Hugh had always charged forward with clear intent.

Needing to fill the silence, he asked, "You aren't considering working for your uncle, are you?"

Obviously the wrong question, and Hector looked none too pleased. The camaraderie growing between them fizzled like stale soda. A pity, since they'd been enjoying each other's company.

His gloom returning, Hector cleared the table.

From the sink, he said, "Hugh, you're a piece of work. Why would you even *think* I'm cut out for the dark side?" On a reprieve, he smiled with wary amusement. "Get the hell out. You're supposed to be guarding Birdie."

"Christmas in April! This just came for you."

Blossom approached the desk cradling a package like a present. Not that Birdie was in a celebratory mood. Surrendering to sleepiness, she lowered her head to the desk.

The drug-like drowsiness should've abated by now. Ten hours of sleep, the three-course breakfast Hugh had whipped up complete with freshly squeezed orange juice— the combination would energize most people. Not so for Birdie. She weighed the pros and cons of sneaking back upstairs for more shut-eye. An unrealistic idea.

This morning the *Liberty Post* was abuzz with activity, the newbies clacking away on keyboards and Hugh barking orders while rushing the aisles like a hyena. He was ten minutes late for an interview in town.

Her cheek pressed to the desk, Birdie rolled her eyes in Blossom's direction. "Someone sent me a package?" A case of energy drinks, if she was lucky.

"Yeah, it's for you. Birdie Kaminsky. See? Your name's right here."

"I can't see. I'm too tired. Do you have a pillow?"

Blossom snorted. "Oh, sure. And an electric blanket. I always come prepared."

"You're awfully sassy for a kid."

"Part of the job description. I believe in working on my skills."

The small FedEx box was placed before Birdie's nose. Too close to see—did she also need bifocals? Maybe the problems with her mother were advancing the aging process.

"Does the package look important?" she asked.

Blossom, who aped grownup mannerisms with remarkable accuracy, struck a dignified pose. "How should I know? I'm twelve."

"You don't look twelve. Standing like that, you look like Katharine Hepburn, curly-haired version."

"Who's she?"

"Never mind. Leave the package and get back to work. On second thought, grab me a cup of coffee. No—two. I feel like Rip Van Winkle rising from deep slumber."

"I'm not your secretary. I'm a journalist. Get your own coffee."

The brew was only a stone's throw away. Three desks down to be exact. If she'd managed to eat, dress, and come downstairs to the newsroom, surely she could make the trek.

Forcing herself upright, she tried to clear the grogginess from her head. The moment she did, she remembered the date. Irritation did its bit to clear her vision.

"Blossom, what day is it?" she asked. As if it were a mystery.

A rhetorical question since they both knew the kid was playing hooky from school. From first period Biology, to be specific. Not that the kid's aversion to frogs swimming in formaldehyde was Birdie's problem.

"Is it a holiday?" Blossom asked, pulling a babe-in-the-woods routine.

"Guess again."

"I give up." The kid rolled on the balls of her feet, itchy beneath the close inspection. "It's not the weekend? I lose track of time. Maybe it's my hormones."

"Don't try playing the puberty card. You know you're supposed to be in school. Where's Snoops?"

"Pigging out at The Second Chance. She eats when she's nervous."

"You're *both* skipping first period?"

Ditching the feigned innocence, Blossom channeled adult sobriety. "These are trying times," she said. "We go where we're needed."

"You're needed in first-period Biology. If there's any breaking news with my mother, I'll send PM on *Facebook*. Pick it up at the library during your lunch break." Yawning, she reached for her keys. "We'll get Snoops at the restaurant and I'll drop you both off. And grab me some coffee, okay? I'm a lousy driver sans caffeine."

The kid trudged off muttering something about stink monsters or stinky moments—was it time to schedule a hearing test? Birdie hunted beneath the desk for her shoes, wishing they were slippers. The big, fluffy kind Ethel Lynn favored with bunny ears and soft insoles. She wore them at The Second Chance whenever her bunions gave her a hard time.

Finally Birdie remembered the package.

Beneath wadded sheets of the *Liberty Post* lay a cheap cell phone, the kind her mother used to stay in touch. No note. Not that one was necessary.

The sight snapped Birdie awake.

Breathless, she shoved the phone into her pocket. Her desperate gaze scanned the crowded newsroom. Hugh was gone, late for his interview.

Don't tell him.

The rule was absolute. Outsiders were never privy to messages between the Kaminskys. Con artists and thieves who didn't protect each other risked the full force of retribution. Only Birdie wouldn't suffer—she'd made the man she loved a target. She'd made him a target *because* she loved him.

181

Mention the phone to Hugh, and Wish would know. She'd know, and do something to hurt him. Wipe out his bank accounts, burrow back into the computers and crash the *Post* ten minutes before deadline—she'd injure Hugh in ways that wouldn't heal quickly. Or she'd go farther, targeting his retired parents or his sisters; a sinister possibility, given how deeply Hugh cared about his family.

And Wish planned to call, a prospect even more distressing. When? And why?

There was no time to figure it out. One of the newbies, Betsy something-or-other, ran to Birdie's desk. "There's chatter on the police scanner," she said. "We have to get to Liberty Square—*now.*"

The vans were all the same.

Four total, tan in color, with squares of cardboard taped to the windows. Only a sliver of glass in front of each driver was left open.

Snoops jammed half of a pancake into her mouth. Like a sleepwalker, she got up from the table, grabbed her crutches, and hobbled toward the picture window.

The Second Chance was jammed with diners, crabby toddlers and stodgy businessmen, flustered moms and high school students snatching a quick bite before high-tailing it to school. They didn't notice the vans rolling to a stop, two on each side of The Square.

In the van parking before the antique store next to the restaurant, the driver wore dark sunglasses and a stocking cap pulled down past his ears. It didn't take a genius to deduce he was masking his features.

Criminals hid their faces. They hid their faces before robbing banks or convenience stores. Snoops had seen it on TV, the scary surveillance videos played endlessly after a crime.

Chilled by the thought, she looked helplessly at the

diners. One of the part-time waitresses was taking an order at table thirteen. Delia was weaving through the aisle with a platter of dirty dishes.

Snoops pulled her to a halt. "Get Finney," she said, pushing Delia toward the kitchen. "Something bad is going to happen. I mean it—go!"

Miraculously, Delia complied. By the time she'd dragged Finney from the kitchen, the van's back doors had slid open.

Snoops wheeled her attention from the cook back to the window. Goosebumps prickled her arms as men leapt out—three, five, more.

They ran into the antique shop. The driver got out last, the hammer glinting in his fist.

He hurled it at the shop's front window.

A deafening crush of sound broke the peaceful morning. It was followed by a man bellowing with fear or fury—probably Mr. Timmons, the store owner. A woman shopper fled toward the street, away from the mayhem. A sizzling crush of wood breaking and glass splintering as the men tore through the store.

"Barricade the door to the restaurant!" Finney screamed.

She raced past Snoops and hoisted a table into the air, hoisted it right out from under the goggling man biting into his toast. She lugged it to the front. Delia grabbed a chair and hurled it within the cook's reach. After the cook shoved it near the door she bore down on another table of stunned diners.

Her desperation, combined with the terrifying din from next door, galvanized every diner in The Second Chance Grill.

Everyone stood in tandem like well-rehearsed players in the tragedy descending on Liberty Square. Snoops scrambled out of the way as two businessmen carried a table forward. They flung it on top of the growing pile securing the door.

The vans across The Square were disgorging man after man.

They swarmed the hardware store and the bakery, hurtling display cases and destroying everything within reach. Customers scattered toward the street.

In the distance, police sirens screamed. Pressing her hands to the glass, Snoops cried out as The Square, the vibrant center of the town she loved, took the beating of its life.

Chapter 13

It was over as quickly as it began.

The flash mob of looters caused significant damage to four businesses on The Square in a matter of minutes. They were gone before the first police cruiser arrived.

Now, with night growing thick and the town in shock and despair, Theodora wrestled the questions streaming through her head.

She'd helped put The Second Chance Grill back together, moving the lighter chairs while Finney and the others steered tables back into place and picked up shattered dishes from the floor.

One of the Persian carpets, a sapphire blue gem, was marred with coffee stains. Paintings hung ajar, and the portrait of George Washington had suffered a further indignity. During the rush to barricade the restaurant's door a plate of eggs had become airborne. Wads of sticky yellow dripped from the frame. Thankfully the portrait of Theodora's ancestor Justice Postell, which hung behind the cash register, had been spared injury.

Snoops, her purple spectacles askew, paused before the table. "Do you want dinner, Mrs. Hendricks?" she asked. "Finney's making burgers for everyone."

"I'm not hungry." Theodora stole a glance skyward. On the building's second floor, Mary Chance's family practice was clogged with folks injured during the looting. "Ask Finney to make a pot of oatmeal, enough for twenty people or so. Some of Mary's patients are too old for hamburgers this late in the day. They'll prefer something easy to digest."

"You're sure you don't want anything?"

"I'm sure, child."

Theodora's cell phone sang out—the third time in less than two hours. She was muttering choice words when Hector, who'd been helping next door at the antique shop, came up behind Snoops.

"How are you holding up, Snoops?" He took a napkin from the stack on the table and swabbed his face.

"I'm okay."

"Your parents are still working next door. They said to tell you to meet them outside in thirty minutes."

"Thanks."

Theodora growled at her phone, drawing Hector's interest. "Now what?" he asked.

She tossed it into her buckskin satchel. "It's Wish again. She keeps sending the same cursed message, *Earn your liberty if you dare.* Why the blazes send it without setting a price for blackmail?"

Snoops adjusted her glasses. "Because she's mean. Some people are."

Hector tousled her hair. "Most people are good," he told her. To Theodora, he said, "Is Wish still using a new phone number each time?"

"Every blasted time." Meaning it was impossible to trace the calls. Wish made the calls then evidently threw the phone away. The thoughts Theodora had been wrestling compelled her to add, "What if we're looking at this the wrong way? Instead of waiting for Wish to name her price, I should offer cash—enough to convince her to

186

go. It means she'll have me on the hook forever, but I can't let her tear the town apart."

Pity worked across Hector's mouth. "Theodora, you'll spend the rest of your life wiring pay-offs to a bank account in the Canary Islands. Or Wish will have a goon appearing at your door for the yearly blackmail. Give the police more time. Plus I'm still working the case. We might catch a break."

"Save your optimism. Didn't the police release Willet Pearson this morning? I'll bet he was among the looters."

"Probably. That doesn't mean we won't get a break in the case. Wish hired a big crew. I'll work my way out of Liberty, contact bars and hotels in a thirty-mile radius. It's how we first got a bead on Willet—the tip from the waitress at the tavern. I might get another tip I can pass along to Chief Burnes."

Snoops, listening with admirable concentration, looked up at Theodora. "What if the text messages are just a diversion? I mean, it's got you waiting to pay a ransom for the town, right? What if Birdie's Mom wants you to wait for her to name a price, but she's really up to something else? She's pretty sneaky."

The observation was sound. Clearly Hector thought so too. "Good point," he said to Snoops. "Sending the same message over and over sure would provide a smoke screen for her real motives."

Theodora sank into an uneasy reflection. Was the child correct? Was Wish, the diabolical she-devil, planning something worse than blackmail?

"Don't lift it by yourself," Hugh called to her. "Let me help."

Birdie smiled gratefully. Hugh weaved through the crowd in the bakery and reached her. He grabbed the other end of the display case. Together they set it upright.

"How are they doing at the restaurant?" Birdie asked. The last time she'd checked, Delia and Finney were cooking an odd mix of burgers and oatmeal for the dozens of townspeople helping to put the stores back in order. "Did you grab a burger? They had plenty."

Hugh shoved the display case into place then stood back to admire his handiwork. "No time. I need to get back down to the police station by 9 P.M. Chief Burnes is giving a statement. He's asked the State Police to patrol Liberty."

"Thank goodness."

"It might not help—State PD will send a few patrols, but they can't give the town twenty four/seven coverage. Their jurisdiction covers too much area, including two major interstates. But they'll try to pitch in." Hugh grabbed a broom and began sweeping up broken glass. Lowering his voice, he added, "If I were the chief, I'd ask State PD to subdue Ethel Lynn and Theodora. They're at it again, tossing verbal cannonballs at the restaurant."

"What are they arguing about now?"

"Same old, same old. Ethel Lynn insists on spending another night at Theodora's. Not exactly what Theodora had in mind. She looks ready to spit nails."

The disclosure got Birdie's full attention. "I thought one of Theodora's grandsons promised to stay over." She wasn't sure which one. "If she has family keeping watch, why is Ethel Lynn coming over?"

"The grandson? Samuel? He was called in to work. Theodora's daughter Ruby offered to stay, but Theodora won't hear of it. Ruby has high blood pressure and her youngest has strep throat. I'm guessing Ruby's husband would do the honors, but he caught strep throat from their daughter."

"Then Ethel Lynn *should* spend the night."

"You'll get no disagreement from me." Hugh set the broom aside and took her hand. When he'd steered her

188

outside, he said, "Why don't you go over and talk to Theodora? Tell her that she shouldn't be alone tonight, and Ethel Lynn is only trying to help. Maybe you should also stay with them, play peacemaker. Hector will park his RV at the end of Theodora's drive—she won't even know he's there—and I'll find a sleeping bag and bunk downstairs at the *Liberty Post*. After what happened today, I won't get much shut-eye anyway."

"No," she said, too quickly. "Hugh, I'm spending the night with you."

Without thought, she'd latched onto his shirt. Her reaction, and the strength of her plea, stamped something wonderful in his eyes. She was grateful he didn't understand. He didn't know about the cell phone hidden in her pocket, wasn't aware that Wish would soon make contact. No matter how much she yearned to tell him or how much she hated the deception, she'd already decided on a course of action. It was the only course sure to end the town's suffering.

"Sweetheart, it was just an idea," he said, enfolding her in an embrace she'd cherish forever. "I'd rather have you with me tonight."

"Then stay with me tonight. I need to be with you."

"Whatever you want, baby. We'll find two sleeping bags, maybe a tent. Do we have marshmallows? I can't build a fire in the middle of a newsroom, but we can pretend."

Softly he kissed her and she eagerly responded, wishing the moment would never end, knowing that when it did, she'd keep it nested in her heart, a memory to sustain her through the nightmare that lay ahead.

Yawning, Chief Burnes drove toward home and the salvation of the chicken soup his wife had promised to have waiting for him.

Since the Kaminsky woman's first criminal act in the town he was charged to protect, the chief hadn't slept more than a few hours each night. He was entrusted with maintaining the law in his town, and he took the responsibility seriously. Pots of coffee at 4 A.M., a staff of officers on edge and evenings spent in endless meetings— including this latest one, with the State PD—had worn him out like nothing he'd ever before experienced.

Driving east from The Square, he caught himself nodding off. Blackness rolled through his vision. He fought it off.

Easing down to 35 mph, he rolled down the window and took in a lungful of air. The air smelled fresh and the residential streets were quiet. He considered pulling over for a quick nap. It was near 11 P.M. and no one would notice the patrol car once he doused the lights. Yet two miles from home seemed too close even if his head was as foggy as Lake Erie's beaches before a storm.

Another lungful of air, and he accelerated carefully. His chin tipped toward the steering wheel. He snapped it back up.

It was the last thing he remembered.

His Honda careened into an electrical pole. Ten minutes later he'd awake with a painful goose egg growing on his forehead and a bellyful of self-recrimination.

The accident knocked out the electricity in the area, sending five streets east of Liberty Square into darkness.

The Second Chance Grill was put back in order despite the argument growing in volume.

"Theodora, do you know what you've done?" Ethel Lynn, at wit's end, yanked dramatically on her gold-studded earlobe. "You've been shouting so long, I believe I've lost all hearing on my left side. Pipe down! I'm coming over tonight, and that's final."

"Go deaf, for all I care," Theodora replied. "As for where you sleep, do it anywhere but my house. I'm not running a bed and breakfast."

"Oh, I wish anyone else would do. You're stuck with me. The least you can do is show gratitude. I'm not expecting chocolate and a Valentine. A simple 'thank you' will suffice."

"I don't need your company tonight. Haven't you bothered me enough?"

A crisp reply wasn't necessary. Glory be, someone Theodora would listen to was striding across the center green. Birdie hopped the curb and hurried across the cobblestone walk.

As soon as she'd entered, Ethel Lynn steered her toward her mulish relative. Birdie caught on fast, her mien growing steely. She'd brook no argument.

"I'm taking you both to Theodora's house," she said, retrieving the buckskin satchel from the center of the table, as if taking possession of the old goat's bag had settled the matter. "If you insist on squabbling all night, I'll stay until you fall asleep. Then if it's all the same to you, I'll go home. I want to stay with Hugh tonight."

Theodora stood. "There's no need for you to drive anyone. You're tuckered out. You've got less color in your cheeks than a corpse. Go on, now."

"I need to stop at home to pack a few things," Ethel Lynn said, drawing her arms through the sleeves of her peach-hued sweater. Battling with her nemesis had brought on a headache, and she made a mental note to pack aspirin. Digging through Theodora's medicine cabinet, which might contain fishing hooks or hunting knives, wasn't appealing. "Theodora, I'll meet you at your house in twenty minutes. Tea would be nice. With honey, if you have it."

"Why don't you pack yourself off to bed at your own residence?"

Birdie slipped between the two. "It's late and we're all tired. Theodora, please. For once in your life, will you go along to get along?"

Finney, wiping down a nearby table put in, "That would be a first." She stopped wiping and gave Birdie the once-over. "Need a snack before you hit the road? You're so pale, you look anemic."

"I'll muddle through."

"Doesn't look like it."

The cook sniffed the air like a hound dog catching something amiss. Ethel Lynn remembered the mangy hound Theodora owned a decade ago, Banjo. The rascal had possessed fearsome olfactory senses. Once the awful dog, slipping its leash at the other end of the center green, threw Ethel Lynn clean off her feet. She'd cooked bacon that morning and Banjo had picked up the scent.

Finney sniffed the air in a similar fashion, like she'd spooked a rabbit from its warren.

Setting her sights, she threw down the rag. "Birdie Kaminsky, tell me what's wrong," she said, stalking over to the table and cornering her skittish prey. "You've got that look in your eyes. Don't think I don't see it—you're anxious about something. What is it?"

The demand shook fear through Birdie's wrists, and she clamped her arms tight to her sides. Her pretty mouth worked every which way, but no words came.

Not that Finney cared. Evidently she'd come to a conclusion. "It's not your fault," she said, making an angry wave at the center green where plastic bags stuffed with garbage, the carnage from the looters, sat waiting for the morning pick-up. "Do you think anyone in town blames you for what your mother did? They don't. You're one of us now, a member of our community. Those madmen who came through today, destroying property and scaring the living daylights out of folks—*it's not your fault*. If you're worrying yourself sick, stop this instant."

192

To Ethel Lynn's way of thinking, affection delivered like a blow in a boxing match wasn't necessary. Still, there was no denying Birdie appreciated Finney's soliloquy. Tears filled her violet eyes, filled them up and streamed down her cheeks.

Her reaction banished the sizzle on Theodora's face, replacing it with concern. "Finney's right, child." She took Birdie's fingers loosely in hers. "Don't I always say you fret over the damnedest things?"

Birdie rubbed her nose. "You do say that," she said, her voice fluid. "All the time."

"Is Hugh waiting for you?"

"He's at the police station. I'm sure he's almost done."

"Put today's nonsense out of your mind. You're a good woman, finest type of woman I know. Why, I'd never have a lick of fun if you hadn't come into my life. Have I ever told you? If I haven't, I should have."

What happened next surprised Ethel Lynn nearly as much as Jimmy Carter's election back in 1977. Birdie, her emotions so pronounced they seemed to carry the taste of honey, collapsed into the arms of her plucky relative. They rocked together for a long moment, the tall, slender girl and the petite firebrand who ruled Liberty like a cowboy emperor. Birdie's affection did something marvelous to the titan's face, filling every line and crevice with an ocean's worth of love.

Chapter 14

Ethel Lynn parked in her driveway, silenced the engine and set her feet on the ground. Immediately she noticed something amiss.

In the laundry room facing the back of her house, the safety light wasn't on. Nor was the lantern above her garage. Leaving her car door ajar to illuminate the pavement, she peered down the street. Every house was dark.

Bill and Emily Dodson, two doors down, never remembered to douse their porch lights. It wasn't courteous to leave 100-watt bulbs blazing into your neighbor's living rooms until the wee hours of the morning, but the Dodsons had teenagers out cavorting at all hours. Next door, the tiny lamp that stood in Bitsy Lincoln's kitchen was also out.

A loud *thump* whirled Ethel Lynn around.

Identifying the origin of the sound proved impossible. Was it from the backyard or the house? Unsure, she scrambled for the keys and took a breathless step inside.

An impenetrable sea of black greeted her in the narrow hallway leading to the kitchen. She managed her way through, and into the laundry room. Padding her hands along the wall, she reached a cool surface—the washing machine—and released a sigh of relief. Past the dryer, she found the drawer where she kept supplies, including a candle and matches.

Another *thump* and her heart scuttled. It had come from inside the house. Given what had befallen the shop owners on The Square, the possibility of intruders couldn't be discounted. Was someone inside the house? She rattled a match from the box and wondered if she should flee outside.

Under the best of circumstances, she didn't have nerves of steel. The thought of marauders in her house, her beloved home with the treasured china and the walnut dining room furniture handed down by generations of Percibles—no, the possibility was too appalling to contemplate.

The settee in the living room with the needlepoint design of rosebuds, the oriental vase on the mantle, the crystal candlesticks and the pewter bowls—every room held cherished objects. If anything happened to the Percible legacy, how would she forgive herself?

Drawing on her flimsy courage, she struck the match. Her fingers fluttering, she lit the candle.

And came face-to-face with a villain in a ski mask.

Ethel Lynn tried to scream. When it dawned she'd lost her voice—and as the villain advanced with eyes gleaming with amusement or deviltry or both—she leapt for the only defense that arrived in her admittedly featherbrained head.

She threw the candle.

Driving through the velvet night, Hugh counted off the houses shrouded in darkness. Two streets then three, and not one illuminated. He was still trying to figure it out when the distant blare of an ambulance startled him. The sound grew faint, a high pitched whine heading away from him and toward The Square.

A traffic accident? He hoped not. The town had endured enough for one day.

A journalist's instinct nearly compelled him to turn around to investigate, but he was worn out from the day's events. He'd handed over the night shift to the eager newbies. They were still interviewing shop owners targeted earlier today as well as the Liberty PD about strategies law enforcement would employ to hunt down Wish and her crew. Several police units from nearby communities had agreed to help, and State Troopers were already on patrol.

Tomorrow would be another heavy news day. He wanted nothing more than to return home to Birdie and grab a few hours of shut-eye.

Yet at the curb before Ethel Lynn's house, he found himself slowing the car to a crawl. Her home was dark from what he assumed was a power outage. Hugh craned his neck. In the driveway, the door to her car hung open.

It was a surprising discovery. Ethel Lynn was high-strung and cautious. She kept a zippered wallet in her purse and had deadbolts on the front and back doors of her residence. She would never leave her open car unattended.

He climbed out of his car.

The acrid scent of smoke hit his nostrils. A second gulp of foul air, and he was certain a fire blazed inside. A fearful surge of adrenaline shot through his body.

The back door was ajar. Sprinting, he paused only to feel along the door —no heat—and call 911.

Smoke spilled out as he threw the door open. Inside, the rooms were awash with black and grey. He managed to stumble down a narrow hallway. The floor, barely visible, rippled like grey snakes. The ceiling was worse; a swirling mass of lung-constricting grey smoke.

Flecks of ash stung his eyes. Stifling his panic, he grabbed for something on the kitchen table, a dishtowel or clothing he couldn't make out.

"Ethel Lynn, where are you?" he shouted. Coughing, he pressed the cloth to his mouth. An awful hum raced across the walls. It was followed by the crackling of wood devoured by flame.

Get out.

He stole a glance behind, at the wall of smoke erasing his path to safety.

Get out now.

He knew with frightening certainty she was somewhere inside. "Ethel Lynn! Can you hear me?" If he didn't find her, she'd die before the fire department arrived.

Choking, he careened into the wall. Eyes shut, he took clumsy steps forward. Shuddering coughs shook him. A few more steps.

He nearly fell over Ethel Lynn. She was curled in a ball, unconscious in the doorway to her laundry room.

The distant blare of the fire engine shook the house. Flames licked the wall to his left, the orange glow reflecting off Ethel Lynn's huddled form.

He scooped her up and staggered for the door.

Chapter 15

Try as she might, Birdie couldn't latch onto Dr. Mary Chance's words. She remained silent as Theodora and Finney peppered the unflappable doctor with questions about the patients now in her care.

Birdie looked across the crowded ER to the doors leading to the surgical unit. The hospital's burn specialist was still treating Ethel Lynn.

By comparison Hugh had been lucky. A few cuts and bruises, and a mild case of smoke inhalation. He was in transit to a room on the hospital's third floor.

Reflecting on his courage tonight, Birdie rubbed her thumb across the fine bones in her wrist. It was a new and disturbing habit. Since receiving the unwelcome cell phone from her mother, she'd rubbed the skin raw in several places. The welts throbbed. If she didn't soon break the habit, she'd risk an infection.

The phone lay silent in her purse.

Not that it mattered. She'd had the good sense to set the device on vibrate. Eventually Wish *would* call with instructions, a terse list of instructions she'd expect her daughter to obey. Yet for once Birdie would have the upper hand. She'd follow the instructions, to be sure, but only as a means to stop her mother from preying on the town. She'd save the people she loved. Maybe she'd do prison time in the bargain, but Wish would no longer be a threat.

A droplet of blood pearled on Birdie's wrist. Brushing it away, she pulled down the sleeve of her sweater and set aside her worries about the course of action she'd set. She brought her attention back to the others.

Interrupting their conversation, she asked, "When can I see Hugh?"

Theodora and Finney, rattling off questions, fell silent. They seemed equally intent on learning the answer.

Mary took them all in with a soft smile. "You can go up to his room in a few minutes," she said. "He's still arguing about spending the night but smoke inhalation, even a mild case, warrants observation. In the morning I'll run more tests. I'll also see him before he's released."

Theodora asked, "What about Ethel Lynn?"

"She's still unconscious. One of the burns on her arm is quite serious. The burns on the side of her face are second-degree. They should heal without significant scarring." The compassion in Mary's eyes deepened. "We know she inhaled quite a bit of smoke but the extent of the lung damage isn't yet clear."

The news took something vital from Theodora. The vigor dominating her personality dimmed beneath the distress canvassing her features. "I don't understand," she said, her gaze whirling from one woman to the next. "Why didn't Ethel Lynn use a flashlight? She must've known the power was out all the way down her street. She keeps a spare flashlight in her garage. I've seen it."

Finney hugged herself as she swayed to and fro. "Theodora, we don't know if Ethel Lynn started the fire with a candle. It's conjecture. The boys at the fire department don't know for sure."

"Well, it makes sense. She's such a Nervous Nellie,

200

she probably dropped the candle right after she lit it."

"At least the fire is out," Finney said. "It would've made me sick if her pretty house had burned to the ground. Looks like the worst of the damage is in the kitchen and laundry room. No telling what the smoke did to the rest of the house."

Jumping in, Birdie said, "Maybe she dropped the candle because she was scared. If she went inside and found a burglar, or several men . . ."

The rest of the sentence refused to materialize. Of course Ethel Lynn had found intruders. They were lifting the Percible heirloom silver or taking the art from the beautifully decorated walls.

Wish had someone tracking Ethel Lynn as she'd done earlier with Finney. The plan went awry when Ethel Lynn didn't drive straight out to Theodora's house. She'd gone home first, and interrupted the burglary.

Birdie didn't need to wait for the authorities to produce an official report—she was sure men hired by Wish were inside the house when Ethel Lynn returned home.

Lifting the oxygen mask, Hugh croaked, "Help me break out of this place." He smiled wryly. "I'd rather spend the night with you. Not that I could be of service, but I'd sure sleep better."

Birdie sat gingerly on the side of the bed. "Put the mask back on."

It was doubtful he'd comply until she'd gone. She'd have to keep this short. The long goodbye she'd rehearsed was out of the question.

"Your eyes are bloodshot." She pressed her hand to his chin, savoring the bristly stubble. He really needed a shave. "You look like you were out drinking all night."

"I could use a stiff drink."

"No way. Not until you're released."

"Have you seen Ethel Lynn?"

"She's still with the burn specialist." There was no sense burdening him with the details. Instead she nodded toward the door. "Theodora and Finney are outside."

"This late?"

"They won't leave until they see you."

His head lolled, and he snapped his eyes open. "What time is it anyway?"

"Really late." After one A.M., she guessed. She only had a few precious moments to say goodbye. Scooting closer, she asked, "Have I ever thanked you for believing in me? I get defensive, but you're only trying to push me in the right direction. I'm glad you do. I'm a better person because you came into my life."

He waggled his eyebrows, coughed, and planted the mask back on his mouth. After a few deep breaths he removed it and said, "I love you too, Birdie."

"I know. And I adore you. You're the best part of my life."

"Did you know Liberty Square is just about in full bloom? The apple trees by the sugar shack are close to flowering. The other stuff is already blooming."

The change of track stopped her fingers from their pleasurable journey across his jaw. "I hadn't noticed," she said, leaning in. She breathed him in, needing to commit as much as possible to memory. After she'd kissed him lightly, she drew away.

He pulled her back in. "The Square in full bloom will make for great photos," he said against her lips. "What do you think? I'd love a May wedding."

The anticipation in his eyes was a balm for her heavy heart. "Sure. I'd love that." In another life, if circumstances had allowed—but she refused to let her thoughts plummet into a pool of sorrow. Instead she kissed him, adding, "I love you. More than anything in the world."

"Then do me a favor. Go home. Grab some sleep then come back for me in the morning. It's a safe bet Mary won't let me drive myself home after I escape this place. She's pretty fussy."

Hating the deception, she nodded. "I'll pick you up in the morning."

After Theodora and Finney said a few quick words, she insisted on walking them to Finney's car. She pretended to fish the keys to her rental from her purse until they'd driven away. Then she retraced her steps to the front of the hospital, where she paced for over forty minutes. Finally the call came in.

Flipping open the cell, she tried to locate her mother's car in the parking lot. The lot was packed— besides, it didn't matter. She wasn't ready yet for a face-to-face.

"Tomorrow morning," she said before her mother could speak. "Write this down, okay? If you don't, you'll never find the place."

Chapter 16

"**W**hat the hell. Uncle Nick, *why* are you still in Liberty?" Hector asked.

Even though the sun was barely up, The Second Chance Grill brimmed with customers. There was nothing like tragedy and mayhem to rouse a sleepy town at first light.

Which was understandable.

What didn't make sense was finding his uncle at a table near the restaurant's picture window. He was drawing nervous glances from the other diners. Nick shoveled the last of his pancakes into his mouth.

He took a swipe at his mouth then threw down the napkin. "You want answers? Get them from Spider." He gestured toward the street. Sure enough, the brute was pacing in the empty center green with dawn's first light sending fingers of gold across his shoulders. "He said we had to come back to this one-horse town. It's the only thing he *will* say."

Hector took in the explanation with skepticism. "Since when do you care what Spider wants? He works for you, not the other way around."

"Not today, he doesn't. My boy has gone rogue. We

were in a diner outside Pittsburgh, I thought he was playing blackjack on his iPad, and he suddenly gets funky. Goes into a mood swing. Like a woman, you know? We get on the highway, and he does a U-turn in heavy traffic to come back here. Scared the crap out of me." Nick paused, his Goodfella mien replaced by none-too-subtle desperation. "Hector, how 'bout you do me a favor? Go out there and talk to him. I've got better things to do than spend another day in Ohio."

The suggestion was less than palatable. "He's your goon, your problem."

"I was afraid you'd say that."

Finney stormed out of the kitchen. Hector groaned. She had a rolling pin clenched in her fist and appeared ready to use it.

She halted before Hector. "Do you know this stranger?" She pointed the rolling pin at Nick's face. Without awaiting Hector's reply, she said to Nick, "If you're one of the men working for Wish, I'm calling the police."

"Ease down, Finney." Carefully Hector guided her arm to her side. "He's okay. I know him."

Nick leaned away from the cook's menacing glare. "Lady, Hector is my nephew. We're just talking here."

"Maybe you should stop talking. There's a scary looking man walking around the center green." Finney pointed her rolling pin toward the window. "Nastiest looking guy I've ever seen. Hector, why don't you find out who he is?"

"Already done, Finney. He's with my Uncle Nick."

The explanation filled her expression with distaste. To Nick, she said, "You should pick better friends. That man has a tattoo right on his mouth. I've never seen anything so awful."

Having made her pronouncement, she wheeled away. The door to the kitchen swung shut behind her.

Uncle Nick, who was unimpressed by the

206

interrogation because he thought most women were 'strung too tight', settled back and rubbed his belly. "What's with the collection plate?" he asked, veering the conversation into new terrain. "Some kid with crutches is getting cash from the customers here. If she's selling Girl Scout Cookies, put me down for a box. I love the coconut ones."

"The kid isn't selling cookies," Hector said with thinning patience. He had enough to deal with today without adding his uncle to the mix.

"Then what's her angle?"

"The cook, Finney? She was robbed. Everyone wants to help her out. She won't take charity so they're pretending to give tips on top of whatever they'd usually leave for the waitresses. Worth it, too—she's a great cook."

"I heard about the vandals in The Square. Big story on the radio this morning." Nick looked around. "No wonder this place is hopping. The whole town is on alert. I wonder who's behind it."

Offering details on Wish and how she'd targeted Liberty was a waste of time. He threw down a twenty-note to pay for his uncle's meal. "So you're going?"

Nick pushed his chair from the table. "Gladly." He shot daggers then added, "You're in a worse mood than Spider. Just so you know, if he won't get in the car I'm leaving without him."

"You'll leave him lurking in the center green? Folks have been frightened enough by yesterday's flash mob. Drag Spider back to Philly."

Nick left without making any promises. The moment the door hit him on the way out, Hector went to find Snoops.

When Hector awoke this morning something had occurred to him. He wasn't due to check in with Theodora for another hour, but he didn't want to wait. Hopefully Snoops had the details.

He found her behind the counter with Blossom sorting the donations they'd collected for Finney. Blossom was decorating a large envelope with hearts in neon pink and bright yellow. The more logical Snoops was punching numbers into a calculator.

"Two hundred bucks," she said, noticing him. "Do you think Finney will mind we're doing this?"

Hector shrugged. "Good question. She's awfully proud."

Blossom stopped drawing hearts. "Have you heard anything about Mrs. Percible?"

"Ethel Lynn is in stable condition."

"She won't die, will she?"

"Kiddo, she'll be fine. She might have a long hospital stay, but her injuries will heal." He flicked Blossom's nose, drawing a smile. Then he turned to Snoops to ask, "Can you help me out? I'm hoping you can clear something up. If you remember, that is."

"Sure. What do you need?"

"The wanted poster that appeared on the Internet—you put it up for Theodora, correct?"

"Wanted dead or hog-tied." Snoops grinned. "I'd take credit, but Mrs. Hendricks came up with what to say. But yeah, I loaded it on the Net."

"Why did Theodora hire bounty hunters in the first place?" During his initial interview for the job, it hadn't dawned to ask. "Something must've happened to make her think she had to find Wish, and fast."

The girl reached for her crutches and came forward. "Oh, that's easy," she said, as if he'd asked a question on a test she'd ace. "I told Mrs. Hendricks about the hacker who got past the firewall I built for the *Liberty Post*. The hacker was targeting Birdie. It made Mrs. Hendricks really mad."

"How did you know Birdie was the target?"

"Money was being taken from her checking

account. Just small amounts, but it wasn't right. Someone like Birdie doesn't know how to protect her online banking."

Jumping into the conversation, Blossom added, "Birdie doesn't know how to use checking. Hugh made her open the account and use direct deposit for her paychecks, but it didn't help. They were always fighting about how she needed to learn to manage her money. If Snoops hadn't found the hack, someone could've been nibbling away at Birdie's paychecks forever. She'd never catch on."

"Plus some of her articles for the newspaper were deleted," Snoops said. "Nothing Hugh wrote was touched. I also found weird stuff in Birdie's personal file—new entries."

Excitement bolted through Hector. There was something here, something he could use to capture Wish. "What kind of new entries?" he asked.

"Stuff in her employment history." Snoops pushed up her glasses, thinking it through. "There was a new listing for a store she once worked at in New Mexico. Only someone who knew her really well could've added it."

He reflected on what he knew about Birdie. Last year she came to Liberty in search of treasure. She arrived with a clue—something handed down in her family for generations. The clue had been hidden in a safety deposit box out west. In New Mexico? He couldn't recall.

The details didn't matter. He'd already learned enough to arrive at a logical conclusion. Wish found cat-and-mouse games irresistible. Considering her family lore was built on a hunt for hidden treasure, it made sense. Following clues, the irritating text message she'd sent repeatedly to Theodora's cell, and altering stuff in the *Liberty Post*'s files in hopes her daughter would play along—Wish enjoyed manipulating people like pieces on a chess board. She also had a history of conning men, but she didn't just take their money. She devised elaborate disguises and invented a new script each time, like a bad actor in a B movie.

Was it possible to get her to play along in a game he devised?

Excitement surged through him, heady and strong. "The clue, the one Birdie followed to Liberty—do you know the location of the cave?" he asked Snoops.

She wrinkled her nose. "Sure. It's a big deal around here. Everyone loves the story. The cave is near Lake Erie, about thirty minutes from here. Why?"

There wasn't time to explain. "Where's your laptop?" She never went far without it. "I need you to help me find Wish. Not find her, exactly—I want to set up a meeting."

"No offense, but . . . she isn't dumb enough to meet with you."

"Trust me. She will. I'll get her to play a game she can't resist."

His animation caught the attention of diners seated all the way down the counter. Everyone stopped eating as Snoops retrieved her laptop from a shelf underneath. He took the device from her hands and, needing privacy, steered her into the kitchen.

They headed past Finney and her son Randy, both sweating like gorillas at the six-burner stove. There was a new employee whisking eggs, a girl with short black hair. The place smelled great. Hector resisted the urge to snatch bacon from a plate headed for the pass-through window. Blossom led the way to the table in back.

When the three were seated, Hector said to Snoops, "I need you to send Wish a message, something she'll see quickly." After the fire at Ethel Lynn's house, it was time to catch Wish *now*. But how? Quickly, he worked it out. "You said she hacked into the *Post*. What if you let her get in again?"

"You want me to take down the firewall protecting

the newspaper? Are you sure?"

The suggestion started the kid fiddling with her glasses. Blossom, a true blue friend, darted to the stove. She returned with a plate of bacon that Snoops gobbled down before Hector could ask her to share.

In a reassuring voice, he said, "Don't worry. The firewall will only be down for a few hours. It's a risk, sure. But it's worth it. I need Wish to think she'll get a big pay-off from Theodora if she leaves town immediately. Let's say she'll get all the rubies plus another hundred thousand dollars to sweeten the pie. She'll figure she's got Theodora over a barrel, especially after the fire at Ethel Lynn's house. Wish knows the women are close, even if they do fight like animals. If I were Wish, I'd take the haul thinking I'd come back for more whenever I liked."

"Okay . . . I can create a file inside the website titled *Wish, please read*. I'll put it with Birdie's articles for the newspaper. She's sure to see it."

Which left only one problem to solve. How to ensure Wish would try to get inside the website?

Hector sighed. There was a second problem. If he set up a meet, he couldn't arrive with the cavalry. Someone as crafty as Wish would detect law enforcement from ten miles off. She'd disappear the moment the PD arrived. But if Hector appeared without backup, he'd run up against the men she'd hired. After the fistfight at Bongo's Tavern, he knew not to take the chance.

"Hold on a sec." He motioned for the girls to stay seated. "I'll be right back."

Unsure if he'd lost his mind, he returned to the dining room. His uneasy gaze drifted over the restaurant's customers and finally landed on the picture window. Steadying himself, he looked outside. In the center green, his uncle was gesturing wildly. Spider glowered at him.

Hector let his feet carry him outside.

"I need your help," he said when he'd reached his

uncle. "I know it means I'll owe you, and we can talk about it later. I'll do whatever you want, as long as it doesn't involve breaking the law."

Flabbergasted, Nick stopped gesturing at the hulk in his employ and stared at Hector. "You want a favor?" he sputtered. "Then I set the terms."

"We'll hash it out later."

"Fine. What do you want?"

Steeling himself, Hector said, "I'm meeting with a con artist named Wish Kaminsky. She'll come with backup, maybe ten, twelve guys. I don't want a firefight, but I *do* want her apprehended. I'm taking her to the authorities." When his uncle continued to stare, perplexed, he added, "I need Spider with me. One look at your thug, and the lady's backup will run for the hills."

The spider tattooed on Spider's lips quivered. He pushed past Nick. "No favor," he said, planting his fearsome bulk before Hector. "I'll help you 'cause I want to."

Nick risked whiplash as he swung around. "Wait a second. Why do you want to help my nephew? His problems aren't your problems. I want to get out of this dinky town."

"I'm helping him."

"*Why?*"

Spider gave his boss a gentle nudged back. "What's the plan?" he asked Hector.

Hector blinked. "The plan. Sure. I'll tell you all about it." Life was full of surprises, but the monster's acquiescence shocked him. He'd planned on ten minutes of pleading his case before Spider would even consider it. Getting a hold of himself he added, "No shots fired, no one hurt. We scare off her crew and grab her. That's all. Do we a deal?"

"Deal."

"Wait here for me. I have to do something." He started off, hesitated. He regarded his uncle. "Nick, your mouth is hanging open. You trying to catch flies?"

With that, he returned to the kitchen.

He'd barely taken a seat when Snoops said, "You're forgetting something. You want Wish to see the message fast, don't you? So you can meet with her today? This won't work if she hacks into the *Post* two weeks from now."

Blossom tugged Hector's sleeve. "Listen to her," she said. "No offense, but she's smarter than you. She's smarter than most people."

There was no disputing the assessment. "Snoops, how do I make sure Wish sees the message fast?"

"Simple." The girl's fingers danced across the laptop's keyboard. "I'll change stuff on the Wanted poster. I'll bet Birdie's mom checks it all the time because it makes her so mad."

The kid really *was* smart. "Do it."

The revised poster read:

WANTED: Meeting
With the mistress of disguise
Leap the wall. Message inside.

Gravel crunched in the driveway. Theodora didn't wait for the doorbell—she skedaddled outside as fast as her bones would carry her.

She met Hector on the front porch. "We can't find Birdie," she said, giving him a shake, as if startling him would erase her worry.

"Isn't she picking Hugh up at the hospital?"

"She said she would, but she never showed up. Someone at the *Post* checked upstairs in her apartment to see if she was sick. She wasn't there—and some of her clothes are missing. They found shirts and whatnots trailing out of the closet, like she's packed up and taken off.

213

Lord, what if Wish scared her away? Threatened her and we don't know about it?"

Studying his feet, Hector mulled over all she'd told him. When his head bobbed back up, he asked, "Where's Hugh?"

"Taking a taxi home from the hospital. I don't mind saying he's frantic."

"Theodora, *you're* frantic. Calm down, okay? I can't look for Birdie right now. I think I have meeting soon. I have to get to it."

"You *think* you have a meeting?" Jangly irritation bit her, and she stomped her foot. "What aren't you telling me?"

"A lot."

There wasn't time to give him the fifth degree. She caught something in the corner of her eye, something was out of place. She looked past him.

Midway down the driveway, a second car was idling. Two men were inside, and one looked bigger than Frankenstein. Narrowing her gaze, she tried to make out his face. It looked like the man had . . . ink . . . splattered across his mouth.

"Who are those men?" she demanded. She shimmied her shoulders but the irritation that added fuel to her engine refused to materialize. Giving in to desperation, she grabbed him by the sleeve. "Hector, I'm darn near frightened to death to think Birdie's run away. What if Wish scared her away for good? She could be halfway across the country by now. Dang it all, I'm in no mood for a mystery. Tell me right quick what's going on."

He was spared from answering. Theodora's cell, tucked in the pocket of her bathrobe, gave a shrill ring. On a gasp, she read:

Don't interfere. Let me leave with what's rightfully mine. Interfere, and Liberty will pay the price.

The message stole what little strength was left in

her limbs. She swayed, but Hector caught her. Gently, he steered her into the rocking chair by her front door.

"I have to go," he said with uncommon sweetness, the kind of sugar a man layered on his voice when talking to a fretting child. "Theodora, stay here until you calm down. I'll talk to Hugh, and we'll find Birdie. But I have to take care of the meeting first."

Wordlessly, she let him go. The tires of his car spit gravel as he headed back out with the second car trailing behind.

Alone, she reread the message. Her heart sank beneath a wave of despair. In a flash, she understood.

What treasure did Wish covet above all else? What jewel beyond price?

She'd take Birdie.

Chapter 17

In the center of the neatly made bed, Hugh found the envelope.

His name was written across the front in Birdie's bold script. The envelope was sealed.

A tremor ran up his spine. Reading the contents would be unbearable, like gleaning a summation of his last hour on earth. And what was the use? Someone as secretive as Birdie wouldn't explain *where* she was going. She'd pen a heartfelt note then leave.

Carefully he placed the letter back on the bed.

The room looked unnatural in its pristine state. No lingerie tossed on the floor, no wads of paper or take-out cartons strewn across the dresser or the nightstands—even the closet was organized. The row of empty hangars took his breath away. Half of Birdie's clothing was missing.

So was her luggage.

Heartache barreled through him. He fought against a feeling of helplessness so swift, it nearly knocked him off his feet. But he wasn't going to lose her.

Ever.

The instincts that made him a successful investigative journalist forced him to go over what he knew. Birdie had probably left at first light. Was she running away? Not likely—she loved him. She wouldn't give him up so easily. Nor would she leave Theodora. They'd become incredibly close.

Had she received a threat from Wish? Something to drive her away? That made more sense.

He recalled how Wish, when she'd first appeared in Liberty, couldn't resist driving by the *Liberty Post*. She'd driven Snoops off the road in a moment of irrational rage. It was misdirected rage—she'd been angry at Birdie, furious about everything she'd become. Hadn't Wish originally sent her daughter to Liberty to grab a hidden treasure? Birdie hadn't returned with the goods. Not only hadn't she returned, she'd put down roots in the town and fallen in love.

Surely Wish despised everything Birdie had gained. A life full of promise. Love. A future worth having.

Now Wish wanted to tear it all down. Not the town, not Liberty—she wanted to destroy the life Birdie was trying so hard to build.

Hugh got the sudden premonition, the one that always sent him in the right direction in pursuit of a story. *Birdie is going to see her mother. She's meeting with Wish.* The reason for such a reckless decision was beyond comprehension.

Anxiety settled on his lungs, and he succumbed to a bout of coughing.

He was still sick from the smoke inhalation and nursing a headache. Leaning against the wall in a fit of weakness, he counted the empty hangers that recently held Birdie's clothes, the Saks Fifth Avenue purchases and the smart leather jackets. He recalled the cozy flannel shirts she preferred on weekends, the fabric as soft as her smile when he'd wake her on a Sunday morning with freshly squeezed orange juice.

His strength returning, he marched out of the

apartment and past the newbies working downstairs. Printers hummed and the phone was ringing. Someone called out to him, but he was deaf to the question tossed his way. He walked straight out of the *Post* and into Hector's RV.

Luck was on his side. The pistol was still hidden beneath the cushions of Hector's couch.

The Glock felt surprisingly good in his hand. Heavy, but balanced. He checked to ensure it was loaded. It was. He suffered a moment's doubt—what if Birdie chose somewhere else to meet Wish? He was banking on his girl's romantic streak, her affection for the patch of ground where her life truly began with a Post-it note and Theodora's affection.

Please Lord, have her meet Wish there.

If she didn't, there was no way of finding her. The possibility of losing her merely firmed up his resolve. He needed to believe his luck would hold, and she'd choose the cherished site for her meeting with her mother.

Shoving the gun in his pocket, he headed for the lake.

Seagulls screeched above the lonely stretch of beach bordering Lake Erie.

Birdie let her feet carry her to the spot where she stood last winter. Back then she'd been a reformed pickpocket unaware of how quickly her life could change for the better.

 The lake was calmer now, the whitecaps soothed by the temperate wind blowing from the south. In contrast, her heart was a throbbing mass in the center of her chest.

She'd left the dents-and-bents rental parked on a dirt road inside the forest cradling the beach all the way to the horizon. No sign yet of her mother. There were only a few minutes left to reflect on the life she must now abandon, the friendships and the deep, eternal passion she'd reserve for Hugh until the end of her days.

The surf's gentle music gave her the strength to turn and appraise the forest. To the unpracticed eye the incline leading ever higher to the cave was impossible to detect, the path obscured by thick pines and the oak trees fanning spring leaves in the morning light. Further down the beach, the roofs of summer cottages were nestled amidst the green.

A few months ago when she'd made the trek to the cave, she'd been a different person. Shallow, cynical—bruised by a life drifting from state to state. Inside the cave she'd dug the silty earth in search of treasure but found Theodora's Post-it note instead. She'd found Theodora too, standing outside the cave waiting for her, ready to offer all the familial love she'd craved. Which made burying a lifetime of anguish a difficult affair to be sure, but she *had* begun the business of letting go and learning to live.

She'd embarked on a new life with Theodora's clue marking the way: ***Liberty safeguards the cherished heart.***

It was time for Birdie to do the same, and safeguard the people she cherished. She'd protect them by returning to Wish. It might take a year, or longer, to worm her way inside her mother's network of cons and cruel scams. But the months leading to this moment had prepared Birdie well. She loved, and had worked side-by-side, a crack reporter.

Hugh had taught her how to follow leads, take voluminous notes and build a story without error. She'd use those lessons to record her mother's every move and build an airtight case as Wish devised her next con game. There was no choice but to become directly involved in the next scam and break the law—perhaps many laws. It was the only way to gain her mother's trust and put her away for good.

The prospect of doing prison time filled Birdie with

dread. Closing her eyes tightly, she reminded herself that it was a sacrifice worth making.

The evidence mounted against Wish must be so compelling that none of her contacts, the G-men she took as lovers or the powerful men she blackmailed, could prevent the years of incarceration she deserved.

From the forest line, her mother said, "My, you look bright and cheerful." She came across the beach with Willet Pearson at her side. "Since when are you a morning person? Your skin looks great, by the way. What are you using? Whatever it is, it makes you glow."

"I'm not using anything special." Unable to resist a zinger, she added, "I think it's called a normal schedule, something you wouldn't understand. I go to bed at a decent time and rise early each morning."

"That's new. You've become a Puritan. How dull."

Birdie let the insult pass. She'd forgotten how thoroughly her mother despised mornings. Waking before noon was incomprehensible, and life didn't begin before dusk. This morning's meeting, arranged by Birdie, was surely a hardship.

On closer inspection, it was clear a lifetime of nocturnal revelry had left its toll. In jeans and a tee shirt, without one of her elaborate disguises or the careful application of cosmetics, Wish appeared well into middle age. Streaks of silver wove through her ash blond hair. Her skin was sallow, the lines fanning out from her eyes deeper than Birdie remembered. Even her formidable intellect appeared diminished by the early hour. By now she should've launched a dozen insults to batter her daughter's ego.

I'm no longer her daughter. Not in any real way.

The thought was empowering, like the discovery of flight. The blood tie they shared didn't lend her mother a dangerous power. Wish couldn't hurt her if she refused to allow it.

Willet ambled to the water's edge. When he was out of earshot, Birdie asked, "Is he coming with us?"

Wish laughed derisively. "You must be joking. We'll drop him and James in Atlanta. Earlier, if they get on our nerves."

"Where are we going?"

"I haven't decided."

It was Birdie's turn to laugh. "Sure you have," she said, approaching. She studied her mother's face, so similar to her own yet radically different. Her eyes were cold. Her mouth sported hatch lines from habitually pursing her lips with contempt. "You know exactly where we're headed. You just aren't sure you trust me."

"Can I trust you? I'd like to."

"I'm here, aren't I?" Her voice was suddenly very small. She wanted to escape the lonely beach, race through the forest and back to her car. Back to Hugh, and the world they'd build together if only they had the chance—

"Your car." Her mother's hooded gaze swept the forest. "Where did you park?"

"Right past the trees. There." She pointed toward a cluster of pines. The urge to visit the cave once more had nearly delayed her, but she'd come straight to the beach. "I'm on a dirt road. It's a short walk from here."

"We have a van. Willett and James were quite resourceful—they stole it off a lot in Mentor and had it painted. New plates too. We'll switch to a car after we dump them. I'm working out the most delicious plan—we'll make oodles of money on our next score. Let's visit a spa after we wrap up work. Do you like spas? I know the perfect one in Aruba."

"Sure. A spa sounds great."

"Next month, all right?" She called to Willett. When he noticed her, she pivoted toward the forest. He was still out of earshot, and she added, "The plan—we'll earn six figures, minimum. Now, I understand you're an adult and

222

want a share. It's understandable. However, we aren't working fifty-fifty. This is like any other business. Prove your worth, and I'll promote you. One day we'll be partners."

A bald lie if ever there was one. Ducking into the woods, Birdie let it pass. It didn't escape her notice that Willett fell behind, ensuring she was in the middle of their unhappy group. Did Wish think she'd make a run for it? Evidently she wasn't taking any chances.

A few more paces, and a trapdoor on her emotions fell open. She spotted Hugh.

He stepped out from behind a tree. Amazingly, he was wielding a gun. Her heart overturned with fear for him.

"Anyone moves, they lose a kneecap."

He aimed the gun at Wish then Willett. Satisfied they'd come to a halt, he beckoned to her. "Birdie, sweetheart, get over here."

"Hugh, don't." She swallowed, but there was no saliva in her mouth. He didn't know the first thing about guns. She wasn't sure her mother did either, but it wasn't worth the risk. "Go back. Please. I'm leaving with my mother."

"Like hell you are." Behind her Willett made a shuffling sound, and the gun's safety released with a terrifying click. Hugh trained the Glock on him, adding, "Pal, if you move, I *will* fire."

"Hugh—"

"Birdie, sweetheart, come here. *Now*. You're not going anywhere with her. I don't care what she's done to scare you, she's not getting you back."

At last she moved to do his bidding. But Willett's brother was faster. James rushed out from behind a stand of trees to Hugh's left, his switchblade poised and his fist raised to strike. The sound of his approach swiveled Hugh's attention for a perilous moment, long enough for Willett to join the attack. It was a terrible ballet of fists and shouts that brought Hugh to his knees. James wrenched the Glock away and tucked it in his jeans.

Birdie rushed to Hugh. He was dizzy from the blow to his back, and she helped him to his feet.

The tragedy of his ill-advised rescue attempt didn't appear to surprise Wish in the least. Darkly, she asked Birdie, "What am I supposed to do with him? Do you think I *need* more problems?" She snapped her fingers and the Willett brothers came to attention. "Tie him up, will you? There's rope in the van. We'll let him go when we get to Kentucky. As if I need another problem. I'd kill for a Starbucks." She brushed past and stalked down the path. From over her shoulder, she said, "Birdie, are you coming? I hate the boondocks. We need to stop somewhere for decent coffee. And aspirin. A *large* bottle."

"There's a Starbucks on I-90," Birdie said dully.

"Finally some good news. Where is it located?"

She felt Hugh's attention, and lifted her eyes. The message he conveyed was unmistakable.

"I can't remember exactly," she lied. "I'm sure we'll find it."

"You're useless this morning." Wish flipped open her cell. She searched for a moment before satisfaction lit her face. "Ah, I see it. Not far at all." Her icy tone became saccharine sweet. "Birdie, dear, do you want a latte? I'm having one with double espresso. If your boyfriend behaves, we'll get him something too."

In the clearing ahead, a brown van was parked. They'd nearly reached it when her mother stopped. She still had her cell open, and her eyes widened with interest. What was she reading? It was impossible to tell without peering over her shoulder, something she'd never allow.

Striding to the other side of the van, she moved away from Birdie's curious gaze.

Racing down the highway, Hector risked a glance at the directions Snoops had given him to the cave then peered in the rearview mirror. Spider, tail-gating, was deep in conversation with Nick.

It was a bizarre sight. Until this morning, Hector had assumed Spider's vocabulary amounted to ten words. From the looks of it, he was spilling his life story to Nick, his meaty lips going nonstop as he drove.

The interstate was busy, but the traffic died down as they approached the lake. It was nonexistent by the time Hector found the dirt road clearly marked on his directions by the careful Snoops. The road was bumpy, and large branches smacked the sides of the car.

How long would they have to wait at the cave for Wish? More importantly, what if she didn't take the bait? Hector had no idea if Spider would consent to waiting several hours.

Or all day.

A well-deserved pessimism rounded on him. *This is why I fail at everything I do.*

He'd executed a plan without giving it thorough consideration. Sure, Wish might check the Wanted poster like a kid unable to stop picking at a scab. But not necessarily today or tomorrow. Maybe she checked the damn poster once a week, and only on Sunday.

Today wasn't Sunday.

He stole another glance in the rearview. Spider, unbelievably, was brushing a tear from his eye.

Wish rarely smoked, but she was dying for a cigarette now.

Alone on the side of the van, she reread the revised Wanted poster with a nasty brew of emotions filling her.

WANTED: Meeting
With the mistress of disguise
Leap the wall. Message inside.

Her cunning warned against locating the message inside the *Liberty Post* archives. It might be a clumsy attempt at a trap. Or was it something else? It didn't matter. She'd already packed the van to leave Ohio with Birdie. In a few hours, they'd be over the border and heading toward the next big scam. Just like old times.

Despite her best intentions, Wish let her gaze wander back to the Wanted poster. Was it sent in desperation?

Ethel Lynn Percible lay in the hospital in serious condition. The stupid woman had interrupted a burglary in progress. Why she'd thrown the candle at James instead of fleeing was anyone's guess. It was her own fault her house nearly burned to the ground and she'd come away from the debacle in bad shape.

Her plight interested Wish not a whit. More to the point, its impact on Theodora did.

Theodora was a millionaire many times over. Her closest friends in Liberty were unaware of the depth and the extent of her riches. Did the old matriarch think she must now pay a ransom to keep the rest of her friends safe?

And it so, how much was she willing to pay?

The delicious rumination ended abruptly. Willett shuffled around the van's hood and cleared his throat.

"*What*?" She stared until sweat dotted his brow. Intimidating him was something she'd miss. He was like a dog waiting to be kicked.

"We got him tied up," Willett said. "You ready?"

She hurled the keys at his head. Scrambling, he caught them before they hit the ground. "Drive the first stretch," Wish instructed. "I want to catch up with my daughter."

"She's sitting with the reporter. Says she won't move."

"Like that's going to happen. Toss him in back. I'm with Birdie."

Sliding open the van's door, she reminded herself of what mattered. She'd come to Liberty to make Theodora's life hell and for the amusement of raking good people over the coals. But mostly she'd come to reclaim her daughter.

Naturally she'd won. Why bother with Theodora's message?

◞

"Touch him again, and I'll knock you out cold," Birdie said, with heat. She looked from James, manhandling Hugh, to Wish. "Mother, tell him to let go. I'll help Hugh get in back."

"You're not sitting with him," Wish said.

"Why do you care *where* I sit?"

A frightening impatience glossed her mother's face. Sensing danger, Birdie relented. "Okay, okay. I'm sitting with you."

"Yes, you are. I'd like to get out of this godforsaken state, and we still have to get your things. I hate mornings, and my temples feel like they'll explode."

"My car isn't far. We'll be on the road soon."

Wish murmured a few words to James. He let Hugh go. Gingerly, Birdie helped Hugh climb into the back, an awkward proposition with his hands bound tightly.

When they were alone, he muttered, "I'm sorry I messed up. I would've thought a gun could take a switchblade any day." He let her ease him down amidst the luggage stacked on either side.

"Remind me never to let you play guts poker." Despite their dour predicament, she chuckled. "Not that you don't have guts."

"Thanks."

"I love you."

He grinned. "I know you do." He darted a glance at her mother, busy rubbing her temples. "Do you think she's getting a migraine? I don't have a voodoo doll or any pins to help it along. I really wasn't prepared. By the way, where are they taking you?"

"No idea." She noticed a blanket and tucked it around his legs. "Hugh, they'll let you go. Please don't try to follow. I'll get word to you at some point."

He started to protest, but she climbed out and slammed the door. Emotion welled in her heart. Quelling it, she slid in beside her mother.

"Pull out over there. You'll see a side road," Birdie said. The engine roared to life. The sound sent burning tears into her eyes. She blinked them away. The van bounced along for a moment then she added, "Right there. See it? Take that road."

"Willet, stop the van." Wish withdrew a leather case from beneath her seat. "I need a moment."

Willett hit the brakes.

Lurching forward, Birdie caught herself before she landed on the floor. "What is it?" she demanded.

Deep in her own counsel, Wish unzipped the case and withdrew a laptop.

She got out.

With her back to the van's other curious passengers, she sat Indian style in the forest's deep shade and began typing. Birdie watched, breathless. She remembered what Theodora had said about Wish having talents she never revealed. It was true. Not only did Wish know how to navigate a computer—a device she swore she'd never use—she was a seasoned pro.

Several minutes later she returned and said briskly, "Change of plans." To Birdie, she added, "Lead me to the

228

cave. No arguments, or I'll drop your lover in the middle of nowhere. The cave is nearby, yes? I have to check something."

✌

Hector wasn't sure what was worse, the cave's moldy stink or the way Spider, pressed to the opposite wall like a slab of granite, stared with malevolent intent. The beast had gone unnervingly silent. Whatever he'd discussed with Nick in the car, he'd used up the day's quota of words.

Nick, who no one would describe as a lightweight, had needed to sit. And so Spider, prior to going into his death trance, heaved two boulders into place. Hector's uncle sat on the mess like a king on a throne.

"How much longer is this shit gonna take?" Nick squirmed. "I need to whiz."

Hector rolled his eyes. "Why didn't you deal with it before we got here?"

"For starters, I didn't think you were taking me on a trek in the Himalayas. Plus I'm older than you. Sometimes the machinery is faulty."

"Too much information."

"Says you. My bladder ain't what it used to be."

Hector risked another glance at Spider. "Chill, okay?" he begged. "She'll show. At least I think she will. It's a gamble, right? We've only been waiting an hour. How 'bout I take you out for pizza when we're done?"

A guttural sound rumbled from Spider. It brought up images of ghouls and a creepy movie Hector recalled from high school. He shivered, repulsed.

The minutes ticked by.

The uncomfortable wait gave ample time to ruminate on every dimwitted idea he'd formulated prior to this one. Day trading. The pyramid scheme selling Acai juice. Scuba instructor, traveling salesman—the two tours in Iraq had worked out, but only because someone else was in charge.

I'm a failure.

The truth whipped Hector's brain. *Doesn't matter what I do, I screw it up.*

His ego tried to manage the assault, and failed. He was sinking into a bout of real pathos, a Greek tragedy of pain, when the impossible happened.

Voices, from below the cave, rose up and met his ears.

Nick scrambled off his throne. Grabbing his crotch, he ducked behind Spider.

Two men entered first, and Hector instantly recognized the Pearson brothers. Birdie was right behind them. Hector's pathos morphed into anger as he saw Hugh in the dim light, struggling to keep pace with his fiancé. He looked like a lamb sent to slaughter with his arms trussed behind his back.

In came Wish.

She strolled to the center of the cave. Instantly she sensed something wrong, her arms snapping to her sides. She sniffed the air and tried to get a fix on the danger.

Then all hell broke loose.

Spider threw off the shadows concealing him. Willett and James scattered like ants at a gorilla's approach. They peppered the air with oaths before sprinting from the cave like athletes training for a marathon. It was a safe bet they wouldn't stop running until they reached Cincinnati.

Defenseless, Wish whirled around.

Fear rippled across her face. But only for a second. Anger then surprise took hold of her features.

She angled her neck toward Spider, unable to believe her eyes.

She stumbled back a few steps. "Ralph, is that you?" she asked in a velvety tone better reserved for strolls by the Seine or Polo matches.

Spider wasn't buying. He advanced, ripping away her composure. She let out a scream so high-pitched and startling, Uncle Nick clutched his crotch as if shielding the goods from assault.

She was still screaming when Spider tossed her over his shoulder and stalked out. Time froze, ground to a halt by her howls of protest, growing fainter by the second.

Birdie threw her worried gaze on Hector. "Where's he going with my mother?" she cried.

Nick returned to the rock and sat. "He's driving her back to Mexico," he said, hunching forward and taking shallow breaths. When he'd calmed himself, he added, "I'm not sure how he'll get across the border. Knowing Spider, he'll find a way."

"He's taking her to Mexico? Why?"

"Just desserts. She broke his heart when they were both starting out, a couple of dewy-eyed criminals with the world at their feet." Nick's eyes grew dreamy. "Those were the days. Cops didn't have electronic tagging or GPS."

Hector stared, flabbergasted. "Spider had an affair with *her*?"

Birdie loosened the rope, allowing Hugh to drag his hands free. "Your mother sure gets around," he said.

To no one in particular, Nick said, "She shouldn't have crossed Spider. Now that he's found her, he'll foil every scam she tries to set up. He can't bring himself to hurt her, but he *will* take away what she loves. You ask me, he's still got it bad. Some women . . . you never get them out of your blood."

Hugh opened his arms and Birdie rushed inside. "You'll get no argument from me," he said, brushing his lips across her forehead.

They were deep in a lip-lock when elation, sure and swift, caught Hector unawares. The plan, *his* plan, had actually worked.

Once he got back to town, he'd call his sister in Philly. And his ex-wives—they'd want to hear about how he'd caught Wish. Maybe his plan went awry in the twelfth hour with Spider taking off like he did, but Wish was out of commission. She was done.

The people of Liberty would rest easy tonight with the knowledge their town was off the radar of a notorious con artist. Which alone made him sure—made him positively certain—the Fates were now on his side.

And for the first time in memory, he knew an absolute truth.

He'd done something right.

Chapter 18

Birdie clamped her hands over her ears. The racket of a dozen pneumatic nail guns crashed through the air.

Every able-bodied man in Liberty, and a respectable number of women, were donating time repairing Ethel Lynn's house. The walls between the kitchen and the dining room were torn down and rebuilt in record time. The laundry room, the starting point of the fire, was gutted and redone. A local women's group purchased a new washing machine, and Theodora bought the dryer.

It was astonishing what they'd achieved in a matter of days. Even the second floor, fouled by smoke damage, received a facelift. New carpeting, new paint—even the women in Ethel Lynn's knitting circle pitched in. They divvied up her clothing, each woman trotting off with a bundle to clean in her own home or deliver to the dry cleaner.

Next week Ethel Lynn was due home. She'd find her once immaculate home returned to its former glory.

Finney, thoroughly rattled by the noise glazing the air, stopped the ruckus with a time-tested strategy. She flicked on the small fan she'd planted beside Ethel Lynn's stove. The savory aroma of barbecue beef and fried chicken silenced the house and brought a stampede of men into the kitchen.

Weaving through the crowd of hungry men, Birdie went into the dining room. Together Hugh and Hector were measuring the walls for the crown molding they'd install this afternoon.

The sight was heartwarming. One look and you'd think the men were lifelong companions. The episode at the cave had squashed the competition souring their relationship. They'd become good friends.

Hugh caught her around the waist. "Were you running errands?" he asked. "Give me a head's up if you take off again. We were hoping you'd help with the crown molding."

"As long as I don't have to handle anything motorized. I'm all thumbs."

"Nope, you just have to hold the molding in place." Hugh patted the nail gun in his tool belt. "We'll take care of the rest."

Hector positioned the ladder in the corner and climbed up. From over his shoulder, he asked, "Where were you?"

Birdie dodged the question. She hadn't decided whether to tell Hugh outright or wait for a candlelit dinner tonight. A fizzy anticipation danced through her.

Trying to suppress it, she motioned toward the kitchen. "You'd both better get in line. The lunch Finney prepared will be gone fast. You don't want to miss out." Her excitement refused to lessen and she said to Hector, "Do you really have to leave tomorrow? It would be great if you stuck around for awhile."

"I've stayed too long as it is."

"We don't want to see you leave. I mean, what's the big deal? It's spring, and Liberty is so pretty this time of year."

"I have to get back to Philly and put my life back together. My sister promised to help with the resume. I have a few job leads."

"Did Theodora transfer the money to your bank?" She'd insisted on paying him the full reward for capturing Wish.

"Took care of it yesterday. I'll pay back my wives and ex-fiancé as soon I get home. It doesn't seem right to keep the rest. It really belongs to Spider."

Hugh's brows hit his hairline. "You're giving him fifty thousand dollars?" he spluttered. "That's generous."

"Tried to. He won't take a dime. Says he was happy to put his past to rest."

"Me too," Birdie whispered.

With her mother gone, she'd now embark on a real future. Maybe a lifelong commitment still frightened her—she couldn't change her stripes overnight—but she harbored more hope now. She even harbored more trust in herself, not to mention the love Hugh offered.

Marriage? They'd do just fine. She'd work hard on their relationship to guarantee its success.

Hugh caught her grinning sheepishly at her tennis shoes. When she noticed his appraisal, he said, "I smell a story here." He rocked back on his heels. "C'mon—spill. What's making you so happy?" He wove his fingers in her hair, his touch light, almost reverent. He drew her back into his arms. "Not that I don't like seeing you happy. All things considered, you deserve nothing but bliss."

"And stop worrying about Wish," Hector added. He was starting to get the weird sixth sense Hugh possessed, an unerring ability to gauge her emotions. "She's all right. Personally I'd like to see her do twenty to life, but what the hell. If Spider says she'll roost in Mexico City for good, I believe him. No idea what she'll do, but it'll be legal. He promised to keep tabs on her."

"I'm glad he'll keep my mother on the straight and

narrow."

Even so, it was impossible to imagine Wish holding down a respectable job. Could she pull it off? As long as she stopped hurting others with her scams, who cared how she got by? A lifetime of bad karma had finally caught up with her.

High time it did.

Drawing her from her musings, Hugh tipped her chin up. Their gazes tangled, throwing enough sparks for a Fourth of July parade. "You haven't answered my question," he said playfully. "What gives?"

Did she honestly think she could wait until tonight? "I was at the courthouse," she supplied in a feverish rush. "Second Saturday in May. It's ours, from noon until 2 P.M. I checked the Farmer's Almanac and the weather online—it should be a perfect day." Hugh swayed, and she caught him before he hit the deck. Holding him fast, she added, "You know, our wedding. In The Square. You want to get married in The Square, right? We need to talk about where to hold the reception. Maybe at Theodora's house? I'd pay for festivities but she insists. She wants to do this for us."

Hugh still looked dumbfounded but Hector let out a shout that startled everyone in the kitchen. A plate crashed to the floor.

He slapped Hugh on the back. "Good job, man!" He winked at Birdie. "Congrats."

Hugh snapped out of his daze. He'd gone rosy from his neck all the way to his hairline. Laughing, he spun her in a circle.

"Thank you." He planted a kiss on her as hot as Finney's griddle. "We'll be great together. I know commitments freak you out, but I'll prove you wrong. Every day." He hugged her tightly then held her at arm's length, his eyes full of wonderment. "Did I mention I love you? And thanks. For believing in me."

She sent a sultry look. "Stop it already. I'd rather

you thanked me later."

"I'd love to thank you now."

"In front of Hector? It would be rude."

"No joke," Hector grumbled. He started for the kitchen. "I'm outta here. Let me know when it's safe to come back."

"Hold on," Hugh said. He let her go and blocked Hector's path. "I've got a favor to ask. Will you be my best man? I'd be honored if you would."

Now it was Hector's turn to sway with disbelief. "You want me, *pal*?" He grabbed his chest with mock horror. "Keep it up, and you'll start rumors. People will think we've become friends."

"We have."

"If you say so."

"What? You're planning to make me grovel?"

"It's an idea."

To Birdie, Hugh said, "Get him to ease off. I'm feeling pretty emotional." His loopy grin took her hostage. "Second week in May, right? You're sure?"

"I said I'll marry you and I will." Something sweet rolled through her. "I'm honored to be your wife."

"I'm having trouble believing it." Hugh chortled. "I need a stiff drink. Or champagne. Yeah, champagne sounds about right."

Hector's face brimmed with mirth. "I'm on it. One bottle of champagne coming up. I'm sure the liquor store carries bubbly." With that, he left.

The women cleaning the bedrooms in Ethel Lynn's house came down the stairwell for lunch. Polite as always, they'd let the men dig in first. The kitchen buzzed with conversation and the delectable scents of Finney's good eats.

A mischievous thought as alluring as Hugh's eyes, darkening with heat, took hold of Birdie. "You need proof of how much I love you, Mr. Reporter?" she asked, tugging him toward the stairwell and the empty bedrooms upstairs.

His surprised gaze bounced from the crowd in the kitchen and back to her. "Are you saying . . ?"

"Why not? If we make enough noise, no one will bother us." Odds were, they'd clear the house in minutes. "We'll have the champagne later." When he grinned, eager to comply, she added, "Besides, I can't wait. I need to prove how much I'm head over heels for you. Now, and forever."

And she did.

Do you have a plot suggestion for a future Liberty book? A character you'd like depicted in greater detail? Please contact me on Twitter with @christinenolfi in the tweet (no direct messages, please) or drop me a line at: christinenolfi@gmail.com with "Liberty Story Idea" in the subject line.

You'll also find me at christinenolfi.com or please visit my Facebook Author Page.

If you enjoyed *The Impossible Wish*, please consider posting a review on the platform where you purchased the novel. Independently published books would rarely reach the light of day without reviews from readers like you.

About the Author

Award-winning author **Christine Nolfi** provides readers with heartwarming and inspiring fiction. Her 2011 debut *Treasure Me* is a Next Generation Indie Awards finalist. The Midwest Book Review lists many of her novels as "highly recommended" and her books have enjoyed bestseller status on both Amazon and Barnes & Noble. She has also written the manual for writers *Reviews Sell Books.*

Please visit her at
www.christinenolfi.com

Follow her on Twitter at
@christinenolfi

Also by Christine Nolfi

Treasure Me

Second Chance Grill

The Tree of Everlasting Knowledge

The Dream You Make

Reviews Sell Books

25983699R00136

Made in the USA
Charleston, SC
21 January 2014